Running For The Bench

CHARLES N. GEILICH

RUNNING FOR THE BENCH
A Brief Political Comedy

2006

Running For The Bench

This book is dedicated to two influential women in my life: my late mother, Allie Lou, and my wife, Mary. Both managed to elicit my best, such as it is, and neither should be blamed for the remainder. I also want to thank my father, Peter, whom I do not thank enough for the gift of education he gave me. What I've done with that education is not his fault. This book is also dedicated to my daughter, stepdaughter and stepson, who provide me with writing inspiration every day. I love each of these people very much. I would also like to thank the many people who aided me in the completion of this book, particularly Judge Dennise Garcia. Like my wife, Judge Garcia is a much better jurist than Norman could ever be, and none of Norman's behavior should be attributed to her or any other real judges. And, of course, I must thank my golf buddies, for their companionship and inspiration, even though they consistently beat me, usually without cheating.

This is a work of fiction. Any resemblance to real persons, living or dead, is coincidental and not intended by the author. I know what you're thinking. Stop it.

CHAPTER ONE

Here's how it started.

I lined up my putt on No. 18. This hole at North Dallas Country Club had bedeviled me for years, but I would be its master. Normally, I landed my drive in the mesquite trees that lined the fairway all the way down the left side of this dog-leg left Par 4, but today, to the amazement of myself and my playing partner, Jeff Frankel, I struck a perfect drive, a slowly-rising shot down the right side that drew in leftward and landed in the middle of the fairway, rolling about 15 yards and coming to rest 148 yards from the middle of the green.

To our further amazement, my second shot plopped down on the green and stopped about a foot from the divot it made, a mere four feet from the pin. I was thinking about the birdie as I pushed my clubs on their three-wheeled cart toward the green.

"Well, I'll be damned," Jeff said. "If you sink this putt, you'll actually beat me."

Seven times out of ten, Jeff won when we played, taking anywhere from $5 to $15 off me, depending on how many "goodies" he added to his margin of victory, "goodies" being extra points for having the long drive on a hole, making birdies, pulling off sand saves, etc. We had money on just about everything, including saving pars after hitting a tree (which were called "woodies," of course), which brought up the philosophical (not scientific, because we were two lawyers, not two scientists) debate of what constituted a "tree."

"Norman," Jeff had said to me, "leaves are not 'the tree.' If they were, we wouldn't say things in the fall like 'look at the beautiful foliage on those trees.' We'd just say 'look at those damn trees, aren't they beautiful when they change color?' But trees don't change color, only their leaves do. Thus, there is a distinction between leaves and trees, now isn't there?"

Jeff Frankel and I had been playing golf together on a pretty regular basis for about five years now. Jeff is the kind of man who gives ammunition to people who say golf is not a sport, it's a game. At about six feet even in height, Jeff weighed 258 pounds, and it wasn't the sort of 258 pounds that a six-foot tall linebacker would carry, it was the 258 pounds that a six-foot tall fat-assed lawyer would carry. I knew his weight exactly because Jeff had bragged recently about "cutting down" to 258 from his previous 265. He credited this to drinking two light beers for every heavy beer he drank.

Jeff practices family law, as I too have been doing for 15 years now, but while I certainly couldn't say I got much exercise in my work, at least I made a point of using the stairs at the courthouse whenever I moved between floors, and I had begun walking the golf course on our weekly outings (sometimes twice a week if we could both get away on weekends). Jeff drove a cart beside me, tracking my pace step-for-step down the fairway, talking all the way. If he was self-conscious about riding while I walked, Jeff hid it well.

Ah, but anyone who thought that Jeff was not athletic didn't really understand golf. The game is not about strength, although strength may help, and isn't about stamina, although that might help some, too. It's mostly about balance and body control, and in those areas, even at 51 years old, Jeff displayed grace and rhythm that would make a dancer envious. He easily moved his 258 pounds like a grizzly bear catching salmon in a river, whereas at 42, I moved my 195 pounds, spread over my six-foot-three body, like a marionette whose strings were being pulled by a three-year-old.

And perhaps here I should mention that I know nothing about how bears look when they catch salmon in a river, and I haven't seen a kid play with much of anything that didn't require a battery or a cord in years. I grew up about two miles from North Dallas Country Club, in a Dallas suburb called Branch Creek, in the 60s and 70s, and my knowledge of wildlife came from watching Marlin Perkins send his assistant, Jim, into dark caves to stun the unsuspecting animals into submission with some kind of tranquilizer dart, all while Marlin sold us life insurance from the tent. Clearly, Jim himself was an uninsurable risk.

But I digress. When two lawyers play golf together, or drink beer together, or merely occupy the same room, all topics are subject to debate. I think Jeff and I got as much stimulation from arguing as we did from golf.

"Look, man," I had said to Jeff, apropos of our tree argument, sounding very calm and reasonable, to myself. "Obviously, leaves are part of the tree. They grow from trees, right? If the golf ball hits leaves that are growing from a tree, which they most assuredly are, then the ball has hit the tree. Yes, it may be true that in winter, there are no leaves for the ball to hit, but that doesn't change the true nature of leaves. It just means that 'woodies' are a bit harder to come by in winter. But you must admit that…"

"What about bushes?" interrupted Jeff. "Bushes have leaves, but we don't count them as trees, do we?"

Jeff said this as he steered his golf cart with his right hand and held a beer (a light one, for dietary reasons) in his left. He drove the cart about two feet from my feet as I walked toward my golf ball, which had come to rest in a stand of hackberry trees on No. 12. Jeff gestured with the beer as he spoke, sometimes slurping a bit of the amber-colored water from the can and also veering dangerously into my path.

North Dallas' club rules clearly stated that you were not supposed to drive carts into tree-covered areas (something about it being hard enough to grow decent grass in the shade of the trees without golf carts crushing the struggling blades, I think). Jeff clearly didn't care about the rule. He lightly guided the cart right beside me into the trees. It was interesting how he managed to never run the cart into a tree even though he kept his head turned toward me during this verbal jousting.

"I never said bushes don't have leaves. We've just decided that hitting a bush and still getting your par doesn't get you any extra credit. But that doesn't mean bushes don't have leaves, too. So your argument displays a false logic." I liked the sound of that: "false logic."

"Bullshit," was Jeff's riposte. "I don't remember ever deciding that. The reason we don't count bushes is that they're bushes, not trees. We decided that it was worth extra points if you hit a tree and still got a par, but it never had anything to do with the leaves on the tree. You're making an *ex post facto* argument, Mr. Spiczek." Jeff liked to use my last name in a formal manner when he got excited.

I found my ball resting about two feet behind a large tree of some sort (it wasn't necessary while growing up in the Dallas suburbs to learn tree varieties in any great detail, beyond your basic mesquite, hackberry, and cottonwood, so I didn't). All I needed to know about this tree was that its position between my ball and the green, about 160 yards away, forced me to take a 3-iron and punch the ball sideways out onto the fairway. After doing so, I turned back to Jeff, who was sipping his beer as he sat in his cart, about two feet behind me. I noticed that a thin line of the stuff was dribbling down his shirt front. This was not the kind of thing that would bother an athlete like Jeff.

"Well, Mr. Frankel," I said, slipping my 3-iron into its ordered resting place in my golf bag. "Leaves are part of a tree's penumbra, and, as such, are inherently part of the tree itself, just as the right to privacy is not explicitly stated in the Constitution, but is part of the document's spirit. Read Roe versus Wade. In fact, I believe you will see that Justice Blackmun specifically cited the leaf-tree analogy in a footnote, on Page 24."

"Good God," Jeff said, as he slammed down the golf cart's accelerator and headed for his own golf ball, which he had driven a good 20 yards farther than mine and just off the fairway. "No wonder you charge more per hour than I do. You're the only man I know who spouts more bullshit than me."

Perhaps it was because of conversations such as the one just related that, on those occasions when I played golf without Jeff's presence, I shaved four or five strokes off my game. On the other hand, those rounds were not as stimulating.

But now I stood on the green of the 18th hole, with an easy opportunity to sink a birdie putt and win a couple of bucks from Jeff. It's true that while, on a good day at the office, if I worked on big-asset divorce cases for good-paying clients, I could easily clear well over $2,000, right now this two-dollar putt meant much more to me.

First, Jeff strolled up to his ball, which was resting about 12 feet from the hole, lined himself up, took one quick look toward the hole, and gently pulled back his putter and struck the ball. His golf ball stopped rolling about three inches from the cup, making him good for a par. I had to make my putt to beat him.

I stood behind the ball, crouching down to study the path my ball would take toward the hole. I considered that the pond just beyond the green would tend to pull the ball toward the left, but there was a slight breeze that might influence the ball the other way. The lie of the grass at this time of day was leaning toward the setting sun in the west, though, which brought still another factor into consideration. I thought that the ball would break slightly to the left of where I stood.

Jeff sighed loudly.

I ignored him, lined myself up over the ball, looked to make sure that the ball was exactly between my feet, looked toward the hole, looked at the ball, looked once more at the hole, then, conscious that I wanted to take the club back and follow through the ball an equal number of inches, gently rapped it. The ball rolled forward off my putter, tracking exactly as I thought it would, curving gently toward the left as it closed in on its target, that gaping hole in the ground.

And the ball stopped one roll short of the hole.

"It was an uphill putt, you dummy. You gotta hit it firmly."

Jeff's analysis wasn't meant in an unkindly way. In fact, I would have sworn he had already prepared to say those very words before I had even struck the ball, knowing that I would screw it up, as I usually did when facing pressure on the golf course.

I knew I would think about the putt when trying to fall asleep that night, replaying over and over how I should have hit the ball more solidly.

Jeff and I said we'd meet in the club's grill for a beer before we left. This would be my first of the day, his fourth or fifth. I'd just lost a round of golf, again, to a man who was fat and drunk. Perhaps I should try tennis.

Jeff drove his golf cart to the parking lot, getting as close to his black Lincoln Town Car as he could while still leaving room for him to get out of the cart and put his clubs in the trunk. He grunted as he did so. This was probably Jeff's greatest exertion of energy for the day. He offered me a ride back to the clubhouse to park the cart, but I declined. Jeff always parked the cart right by the back door into the club. To do so, he had to almost run over the little white sign with black letters that read, "Please return carts to staging area," which was a stretch of cement fifty yards away from the door where three dozen carts were parked neatly in four rows. Jeff's would not be among them.

I had already seated myself at one of the small round tables in the club's grill and ordered two beers when Jeff made his way inside and sat down beside me.

Jeff Frankel and I had known each other for about seven or eight years, but we'd bonded during a case five years ago in which he represented the husband and I had the wife. We both despised our clients, which is not so unusual when you practice family law for a living. The clients in that case could, and did, fight over any and everything, from who would establish the primary residence for their two troubled children (when, in my estimation, they should have been fighting over which one of them *had* to take the little shits) to who got which piece of a bedroom suite of furniture that had cost them, new, far less than the combined attorney's fees they had used in fighting about it. Simply put, Jeff and I couldn't wait to dump these people.

That case had brought us together, though, perhaps in the way two boxers develop mutual respect after 15 rounds of pummeling each other mercilessly. Maybe it's a guy thing. I'm sure female lawyers engage in some equivalent operation, but it's probably conducted on a higher plane and involves more false smiles.

Jeff entered the club grill about 10 minutes after I'd already been sitting there waiting on him. I'd ordered two light beers and had taken a couple of sips of mine. Jeff lumbered into the room, spotted me, and walked across the green carpet that repeated the club's "crest" (as they insisted on calling it) in a pattern under his feet. He grunted himself into one of the fake-leather chairs with casters and looked at the beer placed in front of him.

"What's this shit?" Jeff asked.

"What?" I said. "You wanted a beer, didn't you?"

"I've already had my light crap for the day. I can drink a *real* beer now. I don't want to waste my calories on this trash."

"I'm not following your logic," I said to Jeff. "How can you 'waste' calories if this beer has fewer calories than a heavy beer?"

"Because," Jeff said to me, in the tone of voice I'd heard him use in court to explain to an incredulous judge why his side of the argument was the only reasonable alternative, "I wouldn't have had a beer at all if I'd known I was going to drink this. I only drink this to lose weight, and I've already had two of these. Now I can have a real beer."

Jeff crinkled his forehead at me and raised his eyebrows, signaling that now would be the time for me to see his point and agree.

"You do understand, don't you," I asked Jeff, "that what you just said makes no sense whatsoever? I mean, it's okay for you to say it, as long as we both know that you're full of shit."

"I'll drink it," said Jeff, taking a long gulp from the mug. "But you know what your problem is, Norm?"

"Between my wife, my secretary, and my child's nanny, I'm pretty much kept up to date on my deficiencies," I replied. "Do you have a new one to suggest?"

"Your problem," said Jeff, waving his mug at me in such a way as to slosh around its pale amber contents, "is that you're too careful. You need to loosen up, take some risks."

"Do I?"

"Yeah. You're never gonna be a good golfer 'til you just get up there and swing that club like shit, know what I mean?" Jeff asked.

"I thought that *was* my problem," I said. "I swing the club like shit too often."

"Yes," Jeff said, so eager to agree with me on this point that this time he actually did slosh some of his beer forward and over the edge of the mug, producing a ricochet effect that sloshed some more over the edge closest to him. If Jeff noticed the splash of beer on the front of his golf shirt, he didn't indicate it. Besides, the wet spot merely brought together the two larger wet spots spreading on the shirt from under his arms, the edges of which stains were lightly traced with the salt of his dried sweat. And he'd already spilled beer on himself earlier, so what would a little more hurt?

"Yes," Jeff opined, "You do swing like shit too often, but it's because you overthink things. You care about outcomes too much. You stand up there on the damn tee box going through an encyclopedia in your head of everything you've ever studied on how to hit a golf ball. It's a wonder you make contact at all. Sometimes, man, you just have to grip and rip. Enjoy the journey, man."

"I'll try to remember that," I said, as Jeff took one long swallow to finish off his beer. "It'll give me one more thing to think about on the tee box."

Jeff startled me by suddenly yelling over my shoulder to the bartender standing behind the scarred and tired-looking wood-enameled counter on the other side of the room.

"Hey, Tony, bring us another round, some good stuff!" Jeff barked at the man behind the counter, a man who'd been standing there behind that bar for as long as I can remember. I wouldn't have been surprised to learn that Tony stood behind that bar at night after everyone else left, just waiting for someone to arrive the next morning and turn on the lights. Tony's light black, acne-scarred face remained impassive, as always, and without turning my back to see him, I'm sure Tony simply nodded in Jeff's direction to show Jeff that he'd heard him. "And make 'em roadies!" Jeff said. "Please," Jeff added, the one word Jeff spoke to Tony that caused a couple of the regular yellow-faced, smoking, card players at another table to glance at Jeff briefly.

Tony would now open a couple of bottles of beer and pour them into opaque Styrofoam cups to be driven away by us in our cars, a practice that violated both local and state laws on transporting alcoholic beverages off the premises of a private club and against having an open container of alcohol in a motor vehicle. Besides, I hadn't even said I wanted another beer.

In the choppy way Jeff and I conduct conversations with each other, I said to him, "So, I'm scheduled for a stress test tomorrow with a cardiologist."

"What the hell for?" Jeff asked.

"Oh, I don't know, I think my regular doctor is hyper-cautious. Maybe it's because he knows I'm a lawyer. If he can think of a test, he'll order it. I swear," I said, "I wouldn't be surprised if he suggested doing a spinal tap, just as a precautionary measure."

"I had a stress test," Jeff volunteered. "It didn't really work out."

"What you mean it didn't work out? How can a stress test not work out?"

Now Jeff looked evasive. "They didn't get a good reading on me, or something. I don't know."

I squinted my eyes. "What do you mean they didn't get a good reading? Was there something wrong with the machine? Why wouldn't it get a good reading?"

"If you insist on cross-examining me, counsel, the fact is that I was too fat for the fucking machine. If you must know."

This show of indignation on Jeff's part failed to convince me that he was really that sensitive about the subject, but he did change the topic of conversation.

"Hey, did you hear the news?" Jeff asked me, as we waited for our "roadies." "Judge Curtis said he's retiring. Finally."

Family Law District Judge Stephen Curtis had presided over Dallas County's 404th District Court since the Reagan Revolution swept Texas in the '82 election. Prior to that time, Dallas County had been solidly Democratic, although it was always more Lloyd Bentsen Democratic than Adlai Stevenson Democratic, if you know what I mean. Perhaps that was why it was so easy for many local politicians to switch parties when they saw the writing on the wall in 1980, as Ronald Reagan defeated Jimmy Carter, and did so quite solidly in Dallas.

For over a generation now, beginning seven years before I'd even graduated from law school and become a lawyer in Dallas, Stephen Curtis had been dispensing his peculiar brand of justice in his family law courtroom. Stories about him were the stuff of legend and had become apocryphal over the years, like the time he cited a lawyer for contempt for even suggesting in open court that just because the lawyer's client, the husband in the case, had decided he was gay and didn't want to be married any more, that didn't automatically mean the man couldn't still be a good father. According to this urban legend handed down from veteran family lawyers to newcomers, Judge Curtis declared that the lawyer's position was so "patently untenable" that the only conclusion the judge could make was that the lawyer was intentionally insulting the court's integrity by defending a "sodomite." Curtis put the lawyer in the county jail on a Friday afternoon, knowing he wouldn't be able to get out until at least the next Monday morning.

I don't know if that story was true or not, but Judge Curtis was just archaic enough in his views and Draconian in his actions that one couldn't rule it out immediately, and that alone tells you something. And I guess I can say this for Stephen Curtis; he was not one of the judges who switched teams from Democratic to Republican in the early 80s just to get elected. This man had always been a Republican and couldn't understand why everyone else in the county wasn't one, too, or at least every other *white man* in Dallas County. I don't think he much cared what non-white people thought, and he didn't really value the opinions of women of any color, including those of his long-suffering wife, Minnie.

Stephen Curtis was, however, politically shrewd, and he was one of the first to see that Reagan's victory in 1980 portended the winds of change that would sweep so powerfully through Dallas County that decade that, by 1988 or so, there were no county-wide Democratic politicians left in office, including judges. If Curtis had his way, I think he would have forced known Democrats to wear paper donkeys on their lapels so they could be more easily identified. But what angered Judge Curtis more than Democrats were "soft" Republicans, what some referred to as "RINOs," meaning "Republicans in Name Only." Curtis could work up a good lather about that.

"Really?" I said. "I figured Curtis would die on the bench in mid-screed. I had this vision of paramedics pulling his cold, stiff fingers from the wood and dragging him out of the courthouse after *rigor mortis* had already set in. Although, now that I think about it, he may be suffering from a touch of *rigor mortis* already."

"Nope," Jeff said, "Veronica told me he's hangin' up the ol' robe finally, so his bench will be open in next year's election."

Veronica Wormley was Judge Curtis' court coordinator, who had been on the job for about five years now. Her tenure exceeded the average span of time any person worked for the man by at least two years. I know that just since I'd been practicing, Curtis had gone through seven coordinators.

"Wow," I said. "It's hard to imagine the 404th without Curtis. Somehow I figured the state would retire his court number when he finally left. Have you heard any rumors about who might run for it?"

"Nope, nothing yet," Jeff said. "But I'm sure there'll be a scramble."

Jeff kept up with the courthouse gossip more closely than I did, probably because he was down there more often. I had hired a young lawyer, Vivian Hechtner, as an associate about one year ago, and I'd been pawning off more and more of my court appearances on her. I preferred to orchestrate a case from my desk when I could and let Vivian do the dirty work.

Jeff pushed back from the table and heaved himself to his feet. "Ready to head out?" he asked me.

"Yeah, that's fine."

I think the ratio of Jeff's beer intake (both diet and regular) to mine since we'd begun playing golf today, up to the time he pushed back from the table and grabbed his "roadie," was four to one, although I might have missed one or two along the way. I never saw any discernable difference in Jeff's demeanor, no matter how much he drank.

As we crossed the parking lot to our cars, Jeff punched me lightly in my shoulder (not hard enough to spill either of our beers) and said, "Hell, Norm, *you're* a big muckety-muck lawyer, you ought to run for the old man's bench. That court needs some new blood."

"Yeah, right," I said. "That's just what I need. To take a year off from my practice, run for a bench that I'd probably lose because I'd run as a Democrat, and piss off all the other Republican judges while I'm at it. What a great way to win friends and influence people."

Jeff pointed his key at his Lincoln from about 20 feet away and punched a button, causing the now-ubiquitous "chirp-chirp" sound associated with opening a car door. This is a sound that doesn't exist in nature, and didn't exist at all until a relatively few years ago, that we now take for granted.

Before Jeff lowered his bulk into his car, he turned to me and said, "That's what I'm saying, Norm. Take some chances. You play it too safe. You should at least think about it."

"Yeah," I replied. "Are you in for next Friday?"

"God willing," said Jeff as he started his car.

CHAPTER TWO

Some men, when they reach middle age, are compelled to prove their continued virility by having an affair, preferably with a younger woman, one whose name ends with an "i." Others make do with a new sports car or a motorcycle. Neither of these responses is original, but then, really, what's new under the sun, anyway? Don't look to an inwardly-agonizing 40-something year-old man to be innovative; he simply can't spare the self-involvement.

There's also the question of when a man considers himself middle-aged, a concept that has as much to do with a particular man's arrogance as it does with actuarial tables. After all, a 24-year-old man may die before he hits 25, in which case he was "middle-aged" at 12, and then there are some men in the their 50s who would deny that they are middle-aged.

As for me, at 42, I hoped I was middle-aged and left it at that.

Two years ago, I had been presented on a nicely-garnished silver platter the opportunity to have an affair, and while I nibbled at the appetizer, I forewent the main course. A former neighbor from my childhood home in Branch Creek had asked me to represent her in her divorce, and the neighbor, Lisa, was the sort of person who didn't like to find herself between engagements, as it were. Lisa couldn't wait for the court system to do its work before she began auditioning the new Mr. Lisa. As it turns out, I was (at least as far as I knew) the second prospect, but, still, it was flattering at the time. And very tempting.

I had been infatuated with Lisa Van Dyke throughout much of my childhood, but by the time we reached our teen years, Lisa was running with a much faster crowd than I was. (And I mean this literally, as well as literarily, because Lisa's boyfriends tended to deal pot from their Trans Ams while I drove my mother's hand-me-down station wagon to my job stocking shelves at the local drugstore.) To have the great Lisa Van Dyke come to me as an adult, seeking my advice and help, made me feel like I was winning in Vegas, beating the odds finally. That I was happily married to the finest woman I'd ever known and that I was the proud father of the most beautiful little girl the world had ever seen (no, really) did complicate my feelings, true, but Lisa caused me a hectic few months there, a while back.

So, I could reflect with pride as I started up my Volvo sedan in North Dallas Country Club's parking lot, I had proven myself to be made of tougher stuff than the ordinary "middle-aged" man. Besides, I thought the Volvo was kind of stylish, anyway. And its safety record was unmatched. Its purchase had been a prudent decision.

I pulled out of the club's parking lot, let the sunroof glide open, and enjoyed one of the rare Dallas days that felt more like San Diego than North Central Texas. Even though I'd choked on that last putt, I still felt pretty good about my life in general, knowing I would soon arrive at my home, wherein waited my wife, Loren, my daughter, Elizabeth, and some sort of meal cooked by Ingrid, who officially served as Elizabeth's nanny but had, in reality, come to occupy the traditional role of wife to both Loren and me.

Loren and I still indulged our preference for eating out more often than we ate at home, but Ingrid managed to work in one of her Middle America "stick to your ribs" dinners once or twice a week. When Ingrid first came to work for us as Elizabeth's nanny, straight from Colorado, her cooking skills were...rocky. She tried to make up in enthusiasm what she lacked in talent, but after a particularly disastrous Thanksgiving turkey that, if anyone had actually eaten it, would certainly have led to food poisoning, Loren gave Ingrid a Christmas present of cooking classes.

I can't say the classes increased Ingrid's culinary repertoire (tonight, for instance, she had promised us something called "Meatloaf Surprise," which made me think that the last thing I wanted was to be surprised by meatloaf) but at least she prepared her limited fare with a bit more taste than previously. And if Ingrid was insulted by Loren's gift, she didn't show it.

Ingrid did, however, fall in love with the guy who taught the class, and perhaps this was Ingrid's revenge. She'd been dating Gerard for 18 months now, and although he had yet to ask her to marry him, and maybe never would, the two of them lived together, in every way except by the names on their respective apartment leases. This meant that Ingrid was somewhat less available to us for after-hours baby-sitting, which meant that I wasn't too fond of Gerard. I was also a victim of my Neanderthal brainstem view that men who cook must be gay. Which, I immediately reminded myself, was fine, if that's what he chose. But then, why was he stealing our nanny?

Besides, with Ingrid's family living in Colorado, I felt like I had some big-brother responsibility to look after Ingrid, and I couldn't help thinking Gerard was taking advantage of our cute little nanny. When I mentioned to Loren that maybe I should have a talk with Gerard to discover his intentions toward Ingrid, Loren gave me one of those looks that said, "If I had known you were this stupid when I met you, we wouldn't be married today." At least, that's how I heard the look.

So, anticipating my "Meatloaf Surprise" and trying to decide which bottle of wine we had at the house that might best neutralize it, I insinuated my Volvo from the access road into the herky-jerky traffic of LBJ Freeway.

I've always thought it interesting how Dallas-area highways named after famous people took on the characteristics of their namesakes. LBJ, for example, is a huge, meandering monster of a highway that serves the great societal function of helping cars progress around the perimeter of the city, but it could do so in a much more efficient way than it does. The houses, strip malls and franchise restaurants that border it serve the working class, but with little pride or style. Still, however sloppy it may be, LBJ gets the job done.

Farther north, in the more-tenuous reaches of North Dallas and some of its wealthier suburbs, is the still-new President George Bush Turnpike. Presumably, the name derived from the fact that when it was in its initial planning stages, George Bush the Younger was still governor, and who the hell could have anticipated then that the man who let Sammy Sosa go for practically nothing when he owned the Texas Rangers would actually become President himself one day? So, now, does President George Bush Turnpike memorialize two presidents, or still just the old man? Either way, it's appropriate that the ride isn't free; one must pay a toll for the privilege of driving one's BMW or Escalade along its pristine white concrete throughway, and you'll get past the toll booths a lot faster if you use a credit card-like TollTag than if you have to fish around in the ash tray of your Nova for coins. Those tacky enough to lack the necessary funds for this superhighway are encouraged to take the slower byways or just not visit, thank you very much.

Perhaps a "W Tollroad" specifically honoring the second Bush president is in order now. I envision it being more expensive than the first one, and at some point while you're speeding along in your Saab or Audi, you'll realize that the road goes nowhere, but it still costs a lot. All the brush will have been cleared along the road's shoulders.

There are others, like the portion of Interstate 30 that runs between Dallas and Fort Worth and has been renamed Tom Landry Freeway. It's an efficient, direct route between the two cities that stretches through some of the most boring, tedious 26 miles you'll ever see of car dealerships, Home Depots, and Wal-Marts. When traffic is moving well, it's a great road for getting where you want to go, but it frequently suffers from rebuilding projects along its route that leaves people frustrated and wishing for something different. The road signs along the way with the little fedora hat icon don't seem to help the mood of the drivers, who dream of a more modern road built with the latest tools of the trade.

Today, at around 5:30, LBJ was stop and go, and I could see some distance ahead of me the spinning red and blue lights of an emergency vehicle of some sort (whether of an ambulance or police car, I couldn't tell from where I was) which meant there was an accident contributing to the stoppage. This was both good and bad; even though things were bad now, once I got past the pile-up, traffic should pick up nicely.

All in all, I felt content, pretty happy with myself and my life. As I inched up on the accident scene, I saw a white compact car that was much more compact now than it had been before its collision with a large Ford pick-up. The truck was pulled over to the road's shoulder, and I presumed it was the other vehicle in the collision by the slightly dented front left bumper it sported. The little white car was folded up like I'd seen a heat exhaust pipe look behind the clothes dryer once, when I'd had to get behind there to retrieve a stray sock. All crumply and squished. While other states had vehicle collisions daily, and many of them involved trucks and cars, I couldn't help but think that this particular collision had a Texas feel to it. Small car, probably driven by someone trying to conserve gas and be responsible, smushed by a big pick-up truck, driven by someone, either male or female, who didn't give a shit. There was something disturbingly Darwinian about it.

I drove by slowly, both because the cars in front of me were going slowly and because I probably would have anyway. Car wrecks, like disasters of any kind, are inherently fascinating. I mean, admit it, there's a sense that disaster must strike someone, somewhere, on any given day, and if you see that it has just struck someone who's not you, you've got to feel a sense of relief. As in: "All right! Today's not my day! But, hey, I do feel sorry for the poor schmuck in the Corolla." Of course, if you're like me, you might also be unable to banish entirely the flash of thought that, well, you're a good enough driver that you would have avoided that accident anyway.

Now, I was simply pleased to note that, as soon as I had driven past the accident scene, the flow of traffic accelerated again, up to the actual speed limit as I approached the exit to the Dallas North Tollway. Dallas speed limits are a relative concept, by the way. Most Dallas drivers interpret speed limits in personal terms, like "how fast can I go while talking on my cell phone and eating a cheeseburger, leaving my left pinkie available for steering, without losing control of my truck? 70 miles per hour? 80?"

My speed limit was around 70 to 75, and that's the speed I attained as I approached the long, gradual, curving exit from LBJ to go south on the Tollway. I'd made this exit hundreds of times in my driving life, in several different cars, and I knew that in my Volvo, with its Stablized Track Whatever System, I could easily take the curve at 50 all the way through, so that's what I did, anticipating that I'd gun it when the road straightened out again. I liked the way my car sort of scrunched down to take a curve, like a cat gets down real low when it's about to launch a sneak attack.

I was even smug enough in my driving skill to glance quickly at my radio dial and punch the button that would bring up the station I usually listened to in my car, a classic rock station that allowed me to live in the fantasy world that I was still edgy in my musical tastes as I listened, again, to Peter Frampton sing through a guitar.

And that was when the white van, I think what used to be called a "panel van," flashed by my right passenger-side window. Imagine, if you will, how much time it would take to pass a stalled van, missing it on the left by no more than two inches, I swear, if you're moving at 50 miles per hour. I'll ask you to imagine it, instead of telling you, because, like many attorneys, I treat math the same way I do law, which is to say vaguely, giving "probable" answers and ranges. I estimate I actually saw the van for somewhat less than a full second. I think I'll remember it for the rest of my life.

See, here's the thing. I could just as easily have hit that van, causing my almost certain death, or at least dismemberment and permanent disability. And I missed it through no skill of my own. Before the shock set in, I glanced in my rearview mirror to confirm what I thought I had seen, and, yep, there sat what appeared to be an ordinary white van, looking like an older model as best I could tell as it receded behind me. It was probably a work van, like one an independent plumber might use. The bigger plumbing outfits tended to have fancier-looking work trucks.

I managed to complete the curve that took me onto the Dallas North Tollway, but I have no memory of doing it.

I do remember exiting the Tollway at my first opportunity and pulling into the parking lot of a Big Lots store. I remember that my car straddled a couple of parking spaces at a haphazard angle. And I remember opening my door and leaning over, clearing the doorframe with my vomit by inches. Sorry, but that's what happened.

CHAPTER THREE

Hey, I *thought* I heard you come in," Loren said.

Loren had found me standing in our kitchen, where I had two hands on the island in the middle of the room, leaning hard. I also had some Jack Daniels in a glass next to my right hand, a drink I'd splashed over some hastily-scooped ice from our ice machine, scattering a couple of cubes on the floor as I did so. They hadn't had time to melt yet.

I guess my wife noticed the sweat on my forehead because she said, "You're still sweating; I didn't think it was that hot out there." I didn't answer. I just stared at her. I simply couldn't settle on any words to say.

"Norm? Are you okay? You look a little pale."

I had trouble focusing, formulating a sentence, and I'm a man who makes a living by coming up with words to work through, or around, most anything.

Finally, I sputtered out, looking at my drink and not directly at my wife: "I...I was almost killed. I mean, maybe not 'killed' in the technical sense of that word, or maybe that *is* right, but I was almost...[not "deaded," that wouldn't be right; think, Norm, this is important information] caused death. To myself. I mean, I almost died." There, that was the right combination.

Loren came through, acting as a wife should act whose husband had felt the icy hand of death only moments before and had narrowly escaped its icy clutch, only to find himself now clutching, icily, a stiff drink, with ice, in his own hand.

"Oh my God, honey, what happened?" Loren came around to my side of the island, which I was still leaning on heavily, and turned me toward her, putting her arms around me. She said, into my shoulder, "Did something happen on the golf course?"

Well that was absurd, I thought, and she isn't taking this seriously after all. *Did something happen on the golf course?* That sounded like the kind of question your mom would ask if you returned from a bad day in second grade, in tears, and she knew you were upset about something trivial but wanted to make you think she was really concerned, as if it were a real crisis. You know, like, "Did something happen on the playground today, dear, that upset you? You can tell me."

Now I backed up a step and looked at my wife with furrowed concentration. I had found my words.

"Don't be ridiculous. It wasn't the golf course. What do you think, Jeff threatened me with his 3-iron?"

Doesn't she know I had come within an inch, no, less than an inch, of plowing my car into an unyielding mass of metal at 50, maybe 60, miles per hour? What good is a spouse of many years' duration if she has no intuition about something like this?

"For your information, Loren," I continued, "I came within a few centimeters of certain death on one of our city's highways, just moments ago. I have just now managed to pull myself together enough to get out of the car and make it into the house. I don't even know how this drink got in my hand, I'm just glad it did. The *golf course*. Yeah, right."

I have no idea what lay behind my dramatic, righteous indignation or why I was angry with Loren, but then maybe *that's* the good of a long-term spouse. They're less likely to slap you or simply walk away when they know that trapped behind your words is something unexpressed, and important.

"Oh my God, Norm, what happened? Did someone run you off the road or cut you off, or what?"

That was more like it.

"No," I said, "it wasn't like that. I was taking that long curve from LBJ onto the Tollway, and I looked down for a second at my radio. When I looked up, I was passing so close to a parked van that was practically in the middle of the road that, well, I don't know how I missed it. It seems impossible that I did miss it, really. I should be dead now, you know. About right now you should be getting a call from a Dallas cop with some really bad news."

I wondered though, if they would have told Loren over the phone or if they would have come to our door? No, I guess they wouldn't come to our door because, while the scene of my near-certain death was in Dallas, we actually lived in the city limits of University Park, which, along with its even-tonier sister city, Highland Park, formed the Park Cities, bordered on all sides by Dallas, but not part of the City of Dallas. I don't think cops can cross city limits, even to deliver bad news to widows. Would they call a UP cop to do the job? Would the officer knock or ring the doorbell? Would he hold his hat in his hand and call Loren "M'am?" Would she collapse against him? Do people still use telegrams?

"You almost hit a parked car because you were fiddling around with your radio?" Loren asked. "Are you sure you didn't veer off the road because you weren't paying attention?"

What? This is outrageous.

"No, I didn't veer off the road. The van was parked right in the middle of the curve, just squatting there like some roadside bomb in Iraq, waiting to dismember somebody. Well, but not road*side*, this one was right there in the road."

Loren patted my chest and started to walk around me, exiting the kitchen.

"Well, honey," she said, "I'm sure that was upsetting. Now, listen, we're putting off the meatloaf for another night. Ingrid left just before you got home, and you and Elizabeth and I are meeting your sister for dinner. We're gonna be late if we don't get moving, so please finish off your drink while I pack up our daughter."

And with that, I was left to contemplate my mortality alone, in the kitchen. I also had an impending but undetermined date with surprising meatloaf in my future.

Ingrid often left a few minutes early these days, whereas pre-Gerard she would stay late from simply a lack of anywhere else to go. Loren had briefly considered becoming a stay-at-home mom before trading maternal guilt for her sanity by returning to work as a buyer for Neiman Marcus. Dutifully, Loren revisited her maternal guilt periodically over having someone else spend so much time with our daughter, and it probably didn't help this inclination of hers that we both knew my law practice generated enough money that Loren could have quit her job if she'd really wanted to. Granted, her salary and benefits over the years working at Neiman's had grown to a level that provided us a better lifestyle than we would have without it, but we could have made do with less. Like many two-earner American couples, we chose not to. Freedom of choice comes with a price.

I would have preferred to shower before I went out to eat, but today I didn't care. If Loren wouldn't respond to my almost certain tragedy with the proper horror, perhaps my mother would. So I called mom.

Just after mom answered her phone, I got right to the point. "You almost lost your only begotten son today."

"Did you have a bad day at work, hon?" asked my mother, my very own mother, the only one I'd ever had.

"No, I didn't have a bad day at work. I played golf. But…"

"It seems kind of hot to play golf," interrupted the woman who had provided me with life and should have been more concerned about my almost losing it. "People get heat strokes in this kind of weather, even though it isn't as hot as the worst of summer. It's very important to drink plenty of…"

"Mom, it wasn't that hot. You aren't listening," I said. "I swapped paint, almost, with a van that was deliberately placed in the middle of the highway. Why I'm not dead now, I have no idea. I *should* be, I'll tell you that much. My life would have passed before my eyes, but it all happened too quickly. I was just turning…"

"You had a wreck? Were you hurt? Did…"

"No, mom, I didn't actually have a wreck, but I…"

"Well, thank goodness for that. People have to be so careful these days on the highway. Everybody's talking on cell phones and fiddling with their radios, it's a wonder there aren't more wrecks."

Mom went on for a bit about the dangers of traffic in general, but I was distracted by Loren entering the kitchen, where I stood with the phone in my hand, my daughter trailing behind her.

"We need to go or we'll keep Erin and her crew waiting," mouthed Loren to me, in that way people do when they want to interrupt your telephone conversation at an inaudible level.

"Yes, mom, you're right," I said, "it's dangerous out there. But I have to go now, Loren says we're meeting Erin for dinner. I'll talk to you later."

"Okay," my mother said. She, like me, had never been one for long phone conversations. "Sorry you had a bad day. I hope tomorrow's better."

As I loaded Elizabeth in her car seat, a contraption with belts and snaps and roll-cage-like construction that hadn't existed when I was kid (hell, we didn't even use seat belts in the vinyl-covered back seats of my suburban youth), my daughter said to me: "Make sure you buckle me in tight, dad. Mom said you almost wrecked today."

CHAPTER FOUR

Dinner that night was at "Carpin' Charlie's," a seafood joint on McKinney Avenue that could, and did, fry anything. I swear they'd fry the damn napkins and the plastic-ware if they'd thought of it. Naturally, Elizabeth and my sister's teenage daughter, Sarah, loved it.

Fried food is one of the few things that bring together children from five years of age to 14, and poor eaters everywhere. When I'd asked the kid behind the counter (replete with pimples of course, as anyone would be of any age when surrounded by that much grease) if the cook could just grill my fish, he looked at me quizzically and said he'd ask his manager. The kid returned a moment later and said, and you could tell he was carefully quoting his manager, "I'm sorry, sir, but we're really not equipped to do that. May I suggest you try the fried catfish, instead? It's our house specialty."

"House specialty, my ass," I thought, but didn't say. "Fry her up," is what I did say, which drew an enthusiastic thumbs-up from Mr. Acne.

"So, Erin, I almost died today," I said to my sister as we sat at our table and awaited our fried delicacies. "I mean, not in the way that eating this food will kill us all in due time, but, you know, all at once, like 'the Big Bang,' And I mean that literally. It was almost a Big Bang."

Loren intervened in that way that spouses do when they believe they must interpret their partner's ravings to someone outside of their private world. These spouses often wonder how their mate ever communicated to anyone before they came along to help.

"What Norm means, Erin, is that he was fiddling with his radio and almost hit a parked car."

With Loren speaking thus on my right, I expected to turn to my left and see an American Sign Language interpreter relaying the same words to the hearing-impaired. But no, it was just Elizabeth on my left, playing some game with Sarah that involved farting noises. Evidently, it was hilarious to them. (So add scatological humor to fried food as things enjoyed by children of all ages).

While Erin said something akin to "Huh," her husband, John, reacted appropriately.

"Geez, Norm, you could have been killed. What happened?"

Thank you, John. So I told John, directing my words only to him in an overtly exclusive way so as to indicate to the others that they had blown their chance to hear my riveting story, about how this huge truck was parked in the middle of a curve in the fast lane, thus obscuring it from view until I was midway through turning, and how only by reacting with lightening reflexes (the speed and accuracy of which surprised even me) was I able to avoid a certain, fiery death that may have even engulfed innocent bystanders.

John whistled softly, reverentially, and said, "Man, Norm, that's the kind of thing that can change your life, you know what I mean?"

Yes, John was right. It *was* the sort of thing that could change your life. When a man stares down death and doesn't blink, he can't help but emerge from the experience with a different world view than what he took in. Maybe I was saved from death today for a reason. Maybe I was being reminded of my opportunities, and how I'd better not waste them.

Mr. Acne brought over our platters of fried fish pieces and managed, against the law of averages, to set each plate in front of the wrong person.

Erin said to me, "Norm, do you want any of Sarah's tartar sauce? John doesn't like it either, and it will go to waste if someone doesn't eat it."

"I'm going to run for judge," I heard myself say, more or less in the direction of Loren.

"You what?" Loren replied.

"Curtis is finally retiring. It'll be an open bench, and I'm going to run for it. I think I could win it."

"Hey, good for you," John said. John was my favorite person in the world right about now. "Sometimes, you just have to go for it."

"You've got to be joking," Loren said. "Why would want to be a judge? You've spent years getting your practice built up. You don't want to just walk away from it. You're just having a bad day."

That's another thing spouses sometimes do, especially long-time spouses, especially ones who don't understand that a giant truck almost squashed your mortal soul today. They tell you what you really mean and what you really want. It doesn't make the practice any more endearing that they're often right. Sometimes their ability to forecast your actions will cause you to act against character just to prove them wrong, and we call that "personal growth."

"Yeah, I'm gonna do it," I said. "I've decided. I'll start looking into it tomorrow. You know, I've watched so many people run for office over the last 20 years, and I've given them money and all, but I've never really looked into the nuts and bolts of how you do it. But I think I know enough people who'd be willing to help me. It'll be fun. And, what the hell, if

I lose, I'm no worse off than I am right now, and I'm doing fine right now. Right? Where's the downside?"

Loren was staring at me, a chunk of fried-something speared with her plastic fork dangling in mid-air.

John lifted his beer mug and said, "Here's to Judge Spiczek! It has a nice ring to it. And hey, I know a guy who's one of the Republican precinct chairs or something in our neighborhood. I'll introduce you."

"Oh," I said, as I stabbed something on my plate that could have been fried catfish, but may not have been, "I'll run as a Democrat, of course."

"Really?" John said, in the tone of voice a man would use when his best friend tells him casually that he likes to dress up as a woman on the weekends. "Huh, I may not be able to openly support you."

"So, Norm," said Erin, "do you want the tartar sauce?"

CHAPTER FIVE

I don't want to say that Loren was not supportive of my decision, so I won't say that. I will say, however, that she took a little while to come around. On the drive home from dinner, she hadn't come around yet.

"Norm, are you talking about this judge thing because you think I wasn't sufficiently concerned about your almost-accident today? Because if that's it, I want to apologize. I should have taken you more seriously. I didn't realize how badly you were affected by it."

Now there's a half-assed apology if I'd ever heard one.

"No, Loren, that's not it," I said, and I meant it. "The thing is, I may have been thinking about this for awhile, and what happened today just sort of crystallized the whole thing for me, you know? I mean, I don't think being nearly decapitated today caused me to suddenly decide I wanted to start a new career with what little time I have left on this earth, it just sort of brought to my attention something that I'd had in the background of my mind for awhile."

My thoughts trailed my words slightly, and what I was thinking was that, yes, what I was saying *could* be true.

"Since when have you been thinking about giving up the practice of law?" Loren asked me. "You certainly haven't said anything to *me* about it. Do you have any other major life decisions lurking around in your brain just waiting to be triggered? If you scald yourself with hot coffee, will you decide it's time to have an affair?"

"Hot coffee?" I repeated. "No, I don't think that would be the trigger for an affair. In fact, depending on where I was scalded, that could interfere with my chances of having an affair. Maybe it would be more like a dishwasher mishap."

"Seriously, Norm, don't you think you should give this more thought than the time it takes to swing a golf club? Running for office is a major commitment of time and energy. And isn't it still very difficult for a Democrat to win in this town? I think you'd take it very hard if you lost."

"Actually," I replied, "I'm more concerned about winning. The running itself sounds like fun. Besides, I'm in a position in my life where I really don't give a damn what happens. If I win, fine, it'll be a big adjustment to go from hustling business every day and keeping my whining clients happy to being the one who makes all the decisions and draws a regular paycheck. And if I lose, then it will have all been a grand adventure, and I'll be no worse off. (I liked that phrase, "Grand Adventure." I thought I'd use it again). In fact, it'll be good advertising for my practice, even if I do lose." Hmm, that could even be true.

"Besides," I added, "even if I lose, the other judges will view me as a threat to run again, and it never hurts to keep people on their toes. It may not be what they teach you in law school, but a hell of a lot of what goes on down at the courthouse is political. It doesn't hurt to keep people a bit nervous about you."

Loren said, "God knows you're making *me* a bit nervous. And I don't know if it's good or not."

As we pulled into our driveway, I reached my right hand over and squeezed Loren's knee. "It'll be fine, honey, you'll see."

And so the next morning I awoke with a zeal I hadn't felt in years. It was something like the excitement I feel each year with the first hint of fall, and the air smells like serious football. (Which, in Dallas, usually happens in late September or early October, and is often followed by a couple more weeks of summerlike heat). Except this was bigger. I wouldn't just be a spectator, I'd be in the game. The world was my Texas Stadium. (I know, but remember, I did grow up in Dallas). It would, in fact, be a grand adventure.

I put on what I considered to be my best suit, or at least the suit in which I looked best: a dark blue Armani with three buttons, only the top two of which I kept buttoned. With it, I selected a stark white shirt with just a trace of a white-on-white pattern to it, enough to give it a subtle texture. This subtlety was offset by my tie, which was bold red with tiny little blue dots on it. I examined myself in my bathroom mirror from several angles, and I approved. Forceful, yes, but not overbearing. Perfect.

Okay, now, step two: run for judge.

Except that I really didn't know the actual mechanics of running for office. I could discuss politics 'til the cows come home (and here I made a note to myself to avoid agricultural clichés in my campaign, lest I be called upon to explain one of them), but I had never been involved in an actual, honest-to-God election. So, I decided to do what every lawyer who's practiced more than five years does when faced with a novel legal situation. Personal research? No, no, ask someone who's already done it.

So I got the idea to go directly to Judge Curtis to tell him of my intention to run. Frankly, I admired my cunning. I knew enough about judicial politics to know that it's considered good form that, when declaring your intention to seek election to a particular court, or "bench" as lawyers refer to it, the candidate should tell his intended opponent before he tells anyone else.

It's akin to boxers touching gloves in the middle of the ring before pummeling one another.

Now, in this case, I would not be running against Curtis because he was retiring. But, still, it was his bench, both in the sense that he currently occupied it and in the sense that he'd occupied it for so long that it had come to seem as much like "Judge Curtis'" bench as it did the 404th Judicial District Court of Dallas County, Texas. By going to Curtis first with my news, I calculated, I would flatter him by paying him a certain respect to which he wasn't technically entitled, and, in doing so, I might even garner his endorsement of me. Just because the man was a tyrant with a callous disregard to the lives of the people who came before him on a daily basis didn't mean his name wouldn't look good on my mailouts. (In retrospect, I must give Loren credit here for pointing out to me that this could have been where I made my first official political sell-out, a word I tried to ameliorate by suggesting "compromise" as an alternative. "No, sell-out," insisted Loren, "no disrespect intended. It happens to everybody.")

Except that old man Curtis wasn't buying what I was selling, so my political deflowering was wasted.

I drove downtown along Central Expressway, feeling more connected than usual to the drivers around me and the few people I saw on the street once I exited the highway and drove between the buildings. (Remember, Dallas is not a pedestrian-friendly place: kind of like LA, but not as laid back. Here, drivers *will* aim at walkers, just to make a point.) These are my people, I allowed myself to think, my flock, if you will, and I am sacrificing my career and time to help them. Hell, the people of Dallas County deserve a judge who will care about them and help them through their legal problems, God love me. I mean, if they just get to know me, they can't help but vote for me, and even contribute generously to my campaign. Really, when you think about, I thought, as I aimed my car down the entrance to the courthouse's underground parking garage, I was doing the voters a favor. If I didn't run, who knows what yahoo might seek the bench in my stead, and then where would the county be? As bad as Curtis was, I suppose it could be even worse. Well, I concluded, as I locked my Volvo and walked toward the underground entrance to the courthouse itself, I guess that's why this is called "public service." I'm providing a service to the public, and I liked myself for doing it.

One of the security guards at the walk-through metal detector smiled at me when she saw me dumping my keys and wallet into the tray for her to inspect as I passed through. We'd seen each other so many times over the years here at her station, I felt like we knew each other pretty well. (Talk about a man of the people, I thought to myself. I can relate to everyone).

"Good morning, Mr. Spiczek," said...well, I didn't actually know her name, but, still, we'd always been friendly.

"Hey," I said in return, maybe a bit too enthusiastically, as the guard flinched a bit but kept smiling. "How are *you* this morning? It's starting to get a little cooler out there, can you tell? You can just sort of feel it in the air, you know?"

"Yeah," said the guard, ready to turn her attention to the people waiting behind me to walk through the metal detector. "I guess so. I don't get outside much. Well, you have a good day."

"You too!" I said. "Take care now."

Man, this is easy. It's fun being nice to people. And, hey, there's *one* vote, right? This must be what people mean by "retail politics."

I took the elevator to the fourth floor of the courthouse, where Judge Curtis' courtroom and chambers were located. On the way up, I nodded and smiled, significantly, to Rachel

Knutson, a lawyer who had been an opponent of mine in previous legal skirmishes. I'm pretty sure she detested me, but soon enough she'd be playing all nice, once she saw that I'd be the judge on some of her cases. Hmm...I guess an elected official can never really be sure who his true friends are, unless they were friends before he assumed office. That would be something to watch out for.

Veronica Wormley sat at her metal desk in her linoleum-tiled office just outside Judge Curtis' chambers, where she had sat as Judge Curtis' court coordinator for the last five years, making Veronica the longest-serving coordinator in Curtis' tenure on the bench. Either Veronica could absorb emotional punishment better than her predecessors or Curtis had grown less obnoxious over the years. Based on Veronica's slumped shoulders, unkempt-looking iron-gray hair and the...well, I think it used to be called a "pantsuit," that she was wearing, of a lime green persuasion, I assumed it was more the former than the latter. Veronica looked like the kind of woman who could absorb a punch like those high-tech Swiss mattresses you see at the fancier stores in the mall. The indentation would only show for awhile before her exterior slowly reasserted itself and smoothed out, leaving no visible trace of the trauma.

Man, there's a woman who will enjoy a change in her life, I thought. When I get the chance, I'll be sure to let her know that her job will be secure even after Curtis is gone.

"Hey, Veronica," I said, standing before her desk, waiting for her to look up and acknowledge me, which she did by raising her eyes but not her head. "Veronica" is kind of a hard name to toss out casually, I think.

"You look great today. Is Judge Curtis in? I just need to talk with him a sec." I resisted the urge to wink at Veronica, thinking it might frighten her.

In a tone of voice that Veronica must have acquired through years of self-training in passing on information without claiming ownership of it, she said, "He may be in there. I can't say whether he's taking visitors right now or not, but feel free to check."

Good God, now that I'd taken a moment to really notice Veronica, she was worse off than I'd thought. I wonder what her life outside this little office is like? Is she married? Does she have kids? Perhaps it would be best if she weren't, and didn't.

"Great," I said. "I'll just stick my head in and see."

Veronica, having never raised her head during our exchange, found it that much easier to simply flick her eyes back down to the court file spread out in front of her, signifying the conclusion of our conference. Maybe at that moment I had the first portent that my path would not be quite as smooth as I had anticipated.

CHAPTER SIX

The offices of other judges in the courthouse had been updated over the years, bringing them up to some semblance of modernity and style. Judge Curtis' office, or "chambers" as he insisted on calling his room, was not one of those.

The carpet was a dirty orange color, not created by chemical tinting at the carpet factory, but by actual dirt, accumulated since Stephen Curtis had come to occupy this space in the very early morning of Ronald Reagan's America. There is only so much grime and everyday, sloughed-off bits of debris that an immigrant night cleaner can remove when haphazardly swiping a backpack-powered vacuum cleaner over the floor in broad sweeps. By chance, some of the bigger chunks got sucked up, but the little flakes that broke off the bottoms of the leather shoes of at least two full generations of nervous lawyers, crossing and re-crossing their legs as they sat before the judge, had simply been called to the carpet and left there to decompose. Eventually, they had become part of the pattern.

I craned my head into the partially-opened doorway of Curtis' office and saw him hanging up his desk phone. He wasn't the kind of man who said, "Goodbye," or "Okay, talk to you later." Curtis was more of a "Pre-trial's Tuesday, be ready to go to trial anytime after that," and then hang up kind of guy, which is what he had just said to the unfortunate lawyer at the other end of that call.

I know one thing, I thought, as I glanced at the floor and the shelves against the wall that held years of knick-knacks; the first thing I'll do when I become judge of this court is get a hazardous materials team in here to pull all this shit out. This place would have to be stripped to the girders and rebuilt from there. Kind of like when the Four Seasons took over the stinking hell hole of a jail in Istanbul where *Midnight Express* occurred in real life and turned it into a modern place for well-mannered guests. Well, something like that.

Judge Curtis used to scare the hell out of me when I was a younger lawyer, as was his intention, I'm sure. In the last few years, as I sent my associate down here more often and stayed away myself, he just annoyed me, but still, if I were honest with myself, the guy could intimidate me.

Today, however, I felt like a new man because, after all, we were almost colleagues now, and soon he would see me as an equal. He'd probably want to pass along some seasoned advice to his young successor, and even though I planned to run a very different kind of court than Curtis had been ruling for 25 years, I reminded myself to be polite and patient as the old man rambled on.

"Hey, Judge, how's it going?" I asked, to get Curtis' attention in a friendly way, since he hadn't as yet noticed me standing in his door, waiting for him to acknowledge me and invite me in.

Curtis never looked up or turned in my direction, but said, as if speaking to his desk, "What is it, Mr. Spiczek?"

So that was a bit freaky. This court had a talent for perceiving and speaking to people without looking directly at them.

"Have you got a minute, your honor?" I asked, still standing in the doorway but leaning my body inward to the room, signaling my desire to enter. "I just wanted to talk to you about something."

"Go ahead," said Curtis, at least nodding his head toward the two chairs resting opposite his desk. These two cheap-looking leather chairs had arrived here with Curtis himself, I felt sure, and the seats of them were shiny from the friction of so many years of wool-suited asses shifting around on them. I was always uncomfortable sitting on them and tried to remember to send immediately to the dry cleaners whatever suit I'd been wearing when I had to sit on one.

"Great," I said, as I rested my briefcase against my legs and sat in one of the chairs, trying to squeeze my cheeks as tightly as I could, thus reducing the amount of pant cloth making contact with the chair. I'm not even a germ freak normally, but this was not a normal place.

"So, how have you been doing lately, judge? Is everything just as busy as ever?" I asked Curtis. I doubt that my conversational gambit sounded any more banal to him than it did to my own ears.

"Yes, Mr. Spiczek, I am busy. Is there something I can do for you?"

Every other judge in this courthouse called me Norm and I called them by their first names, unless we were actually involved in a hearing in a courtroom. Not Curtis; it was "Mr. Spiczek" the day I had first met him when I was still a lawyer in my 20s, and it was "Mr. Spiczek" today. On the other hand, he never forgot a name, and I never had to repeat mine to him or remind him how to pronounce it, after my first petrified appearance in his courtroom.

And at least when Judge Curtis had uttered these last words, he had finally looked up from his desk to glance at me.

So, fine, I thought, let's get down to it. I'm only doing this as a professional courtesy anyway, so I don't really give a damn about Judge Stephen Curtis and his lack of social skills any more.

"Well, it's like this, Judge," I said. "I heard you're retiring and not running in the next election. You've served Dallas County well for a long time, and it's certainly a well-deserved rest. I just wanted to let you know, so you'd hear it from me first, that I intend to run for this bench. And I hope to do the 404th proud well into the future."

Curtis narrowed his already beady eyes in his sharp head, mostly bald now except for a lowered halo of short white hair around his skull at the ear level. He leaned forward, bringing his hands together in front of him and resting them on his desk.

"Now who told you that, Mr. Spiczek? You're the second person who's come in my office this week to inform me of my imminent demise and seek my blessing in taking over my court. What if I'm not going anywhere?"

Whoa. Where to start with that declaration?

"I'm *what?*" I said. Now *I* was leaning forward, bringing Judge Curtis and me closer to each other than we may have ever been, even though there was still a half-ton slab of wooden desk between us. "Someone else said they're running for this bench? You've got to be kidding. Who is it?"

Now Curtis was enjoying himself. He sat back in his desk chair, making the springs squeak a bit as he did so. He steepled his hands in front of him and actually made a thin-lipped, dry attempt at a smile as he spoke.

"Now isn't it interesting, Mr. Spiczek, that you have chosen to focus on the first part of my statement, rather than the second? Your prospective opponent was more perceptive than you. In fact, she had the good sense to apologize to me when she thought she was mistaken and that I was not, in fact, retiring. She said she, of course, had no intention to seek this office while I occupied it. You, however, skipped right over that and focused on who your supposed opponent is. Perhaps that's why she is a better lawyer than you, Mr. Spiczek. You so often seem to miss the point."

Curtis' nasty little smile crinkled a bit more at this, indicating, I think, that he particularly enjoyed that last part.

What is it with this man, I thought? I had never disrespected him to his face, I had never been anything other than ethical and professional in his court, yet he had always seemed to dislike me, and now he had just come right out and insulted me. Well, fuck him, I don't have to take this. We're not in his courtroom, this didn't involve any case, and I've got standing in this community.

"Yeah, well," I said, my voice getting deeper, but quieter, "let me amend what I said. Here's where we are. I don't give a damn whether you decide to run or not, or who the hell else decides to run. I intend to run for this bench, and I intend to win. And the thing is, it's not even because I really want the job. I'm just fine doing what I'm doing now, and God knows I make more money being a lawyer than being a judge. It's just that I'm tired of seeing you mistreat people in your court, lawyers and litigants alike, just to get your jollies. It's time for a change, *your honor*, and I say that with all the hollow formality to which you're entitled, and I'm the change."

Jesus Christ, where had that come from? One doesn't utter a declaration of war like that without it being the release of years of built-up anger and frustration, and somehow I think it was about more than just Stephen Curtis. But it had felt delicious saying it.

"Oh, how dramatic, Norman. (So that's what it took for the man to say my name for the first time in 15 years). You must have seen that in a movie somewhere. Was it Al Pacino

45

or something? Do you think I don't know how you feel about me? Do you really think anything is said about me in this courthouse of which I'm not aware? I know you don't care for me, you and hundreds of others. But I keep getting elected, don't I? Why do you think that is, or are you so new to the business of politics that you haven't given it any thought? Well, let me help you out here. Consider it your first piece of political advice, and the last you'll get from me." Curtis unclasped his hands and pointed one of his bony fingers at me. "Lawyers don't elect judges, not even hot-shots like you. There aren't enough of you. Sure, we take your money, and you'll give it to us whether you like us or not, because you're scared to death of making us angry if you don't. And you're right to think that. But other than that, *we don't care what you think.*

"Oh," continued Curtis, "some of my colleagues may like some lawyers more than I do, and I know that they inappropriately socialize with you, but my priorities have always been to my God, my country, my political party, and my family. Other than that, I really don't care what people like you think of me. So, anyway, I may or may not retire, but if I do, I certainly would never support some homosexual-loving, liberal, prissy punk like you to take my place. I haven't put all this work into keeping Dallas County out of the hands of Godless Democrats just to hand it over when I retire. And one more thing, Mr. Spiczek, Dallas County doesn't want your type either, so don't kid yourself. We haven't become New York yet, thank God. So think hard about your decision before you run for this court. You might do well to stop before you ever get started."

"Judge," I said, rising from my chair and retrieving my briefcase. "This has been a very inspiring little talk. I'm just beginning."

CHAPTER SEVEN

The first thing I did when I returned to my office and sat down at my desk was to call Jeff. I told him about my astonishing conversation with Judge Curtis. Jeff reacted as a friend should.

"Good God, what a prick that man is," Jeff said into the phone. "He's just given up all pretense of civility, hasn't he? Of course, you should really take this as a compliment, you know."

"Really?" I asked. "I didn't *feel* complimented, I can tell you that."

"No, no, this means you threaten him. His outburst betrays his own words, don't you see?" said Jeff. "If someone else had told him they were running against him, he would have laughed at them. The only reason he got so upset is that you threaten to mess up his whole plan, and he's afraid that you could really do it. He's trying to scare you off. Now, if he were a smart man who could control himself, he would have tried being extra nice to you instead of getting nasty. But it's too late for that now."

"Yes," I agreed, "I would say so. But I wonder who else had already been in to see him? It's always amazing to me how fast news spreads around the courthouse."

"Oh," Jeff said, "that would be Hildy Pierce. I was going to call you about that later this morning."

"Hildegarde Pierce, from the DA's office? *She* wants to run for judge? Is this just another way for her satisfy her desire to steal children from their parents?" I asked Jeff.

Hildegarde Pierce, also known as (but rarely to her face) Hildy, had been an assistant district attorney in Dallas County for about as long as I'd practiced law here, and had, for most of that time, worked in the Juvenile section of the DA's office. This meant she was now in charge of 12 other prosecutors who represented Child Protective Services in cases in which CPS removed children from their parents. The officially-stated policy of CPS, right on the very web site that most CPS parents would never read because they were as illiterate with computers as with non-digital media, said the goal of CPS is to "re-unite" families. Somewhat like President W's "Clear Skies" initiative was supposed to lead to less pollution by allowing industry to police itself. If "reunion" was CPS' stated ambition, it was rarely achieved, especially when Hildy Pierce herself was on the case. In addition to supervising other prosecutors, Hildy carried a caseload herself.

My rhetorical question to Jeff really wasn't fair in that, most of the time, Hildy Pierce was absolutely right to urge her client, CPS, to permanently terminate the parental rights of the meth and crack addicts who abandoned their children to the streets and abusive boyfriends. It's just that, occasionally, a parent had just hit a rough patch and deserved a second chance, and Hildy was not known for being big on redemption, at least in this world. She was also in her mid-40s, unmarried, not known to date, childless, and, thus suspect in my book. She invariably wore a largish gold cross around her neck, dangling down the front of what was often a white frilly blouse with bits of lace at the collar closed tightly around her neck. The cross had always seemed intended as a repellant, at least to me. Evidently, it had done its job over the years. Hildegarde Pierce might be, in some circumstances, witty and charming, but I'd already given her all the thought I intended to and had closed my book on her.

"Yep," said Jeff, "Hildegarde told Curtis' coordinator yesterday afternoon that she felt a 'calling' to be a judge. Evidently, she and the coordinator, what's-her-name, are pretty close."

I made that sound with my lips that leaves traces of saliva on the phone. You know, phhhhh...

"Bullshit, Hildy Pierce isn't close to anybody except her personal Jesus, and *they're* not doing it, if you know what I mean."

"Good God, Norm," said Jeff, "do I detect bitterness here? No one ever said you could just anoint yourself judge. So you have an opponent in the general election? So what? You'll just have to get out there and hustle a little bit, that's all. Besides, *your* reason for running is no sillier than hers. She says she has a 'calling,' which sounds pretty fucking noble, and you, well, I think you gave it a couple of seconds of thought in your backswing. Not that there's anything wrong with that, but you might want to work on the story of your inspiration a little before delivering it to the public. And Jesus, stay away from talking about anybody's 'personal Jesus,' for God's sake. Just stay away from religion altogether. It doesn't look good on you."

Jeff was right. I was feeling something, maybe bitterness. Whatever it was caused me to feel sullen, like Hildegarde Pierce had rained on my parade. I mean, damn, now I would have to actually work for this thing. I'd seen judges at those ridiculous fundraisers, glad-handing everybody, playing the cheery fools, hoping you would give them lots of money and acting like your best friend while they glanced at your nametag. They looked pathetic. I always felt pathetic when I shook their hands and played along. And the undercurrent to all those affairs was an implied *quid pro quo* that was depressingly unreliable.

Still, if I had to have an opponent, better that it be a wet noodle like Hildegarde than someone with a spark of charm.

"No, no," I reassured Jeff, "I'll be fine. And for your information, I didn't just decide to run for judge in my backswing, I..."

"Yeah, I know," Jeff said, "you decapitated yourself on the Tollway and carried your own bloody head for two miles, uphill, in the snow, to the nearest hospital, and stitched the damn thing back on yourself. We really do need to work on your story."

"Whatever," I said. "And I can do the religion thing, by the way, if I have to. Although I don't see why that would come up in a race for a family law bench in Dallas County. I'm not running for President."

"Oh, I think you might be surprised, my friend," Jeff said. "It's hard to have a case with Hildegarde where religion doesn't come up. In my last CPS case with her, she wanted to terminate my gal because Hildegarde said the lady had 'sinned' by having three children outside the holy bonds of matrimony, never mind the woman's heroin habit. And this is after 20 years of her prosecuting these damn things. I had to take the case to a jury."

"And?" I asked.

"I lost," Jeff said.

CHAPTER EIGHT

S o," Loren said to me over dinner that night, as we sat with our daughter at one of our favorite Tex-Mex places, "Holy Mole," "let's review how your campaign is going so far. You've cussed out the man you're trying to replace, who may not resign anyway, and drawn a radical Christian right opponent who has nothing to do in her life but pray to her God to strike you down. Does that sum it up?" Loren asked this as she dipped another chip into the black bean sauce. This was the same black bean sauce with which Elizabeth now had encircled her face, giving her the unsettling appearance of having one of those half beard and mustache things that guys grow when they want to look like bad asses but still keep their day jobs.

"Well," I said, "when *you* say it, you make it sound so dramatic." Loren's response was to crunch her chip loudly.

"What are two talking about?" Elizabeth asked us.

Her voice wasn't exactly whining, yet, but it was crafted as a warning that whining could soon follow. One of my daughter's frequent complaints was that Loren and I engaged in too much adult conversation at the dinner table, which left Elizabeth out. One of the frequent complaints of Loren and I was that we never found enough time to engage in adult conversation. We compromised by capitulating to Elizabeth, like most working parents do who feel guilty about their parental absenteeism anyway.

Loren sought to clear up Elizabeth's confusion by, first, dipping an extra napkin in a glass of water and trying to smear off some of the excess black bean dip from around Elizabeth's face (making Elizabeth sorry she'd spoken and, thus, drawn attention to herself), and then saying, "Daddy says he's running for judge, dear."

Elizabeth simultaneously pushed Loren's napkin away and turned her head.

"Is it a long run?" Elizabeth asked. "Do you go in a circle?"

Kids really are the perfect straight men.

"Yes and yes," I said. "No, not really, honey. *Running* for office is just something people say when what they really mean is that they're trying to get elected. You know, to get people to vote for them. What happens is that two people, well, sometimes more, but usually it comes down to two people want the same job, so they ask everyone to vote on who would do the best. The one who gets the most votes wins."

I said this while leaning down toward my little girl and using my best "Mr. Rogers" non-threatening voice that my wife had trained me to use over the years. Evidently, my "work" tone of voice, as Loren called it, frightened small children and adults with delicate sensibilities. I had taken that as a compliment, but Loren explained that she had not intended it to be.

Elizabeth appeared to ponder my explanation as she wiped the remaining black bean sauce off her chin with the sleeve of her dress, causing an exasperated sigh from her mother.

"Well," Elizabeth said, "I'll *probably* vote for you. But who's the other person who wants the job?"

It had never occurred to me that winning Dallas County would start at home. And it was also dawning on me that my beautiful little girl, whom I had so confidently known was more like me than she was like Loren, was now becoming her mother.

I said to Elizabeth, "She's an evil dragon who breathes fire and tries to hurt good people, and it's my job to slay her."

Loren rolled her eyes and tilted her head toward her shoulder at the same time. That's bad.

Well, it got a giggle out of Elizabeth, and making your daughter giggle is one of the truly great things a man can do, outside of a show of physical strength. The end justifies the means, said my return smirk to Loren.

"Why do they call it *running* for the job, then?" Elizabeth asked.

"Well, sweetie," I began confidently, "it's because..." My gesticulating hands froze in mid-air. "It's because...Well, I have no idea." Children and spouses are ever-ready to remind you of your general ignorance.

Loren wanted to return to a serious conversation.

"Isn't your practice awfully busy right now," Loren asked me. "That's what you were saying last week, about how stressed out you are and you have too much work to do. How are you going to handle that while you do this election thing, too?"

So now it's "an election thing."

"Well," I said, "as a matter of fact, I had my stress test today, and the cardiologist said that my heart was perfectly normal for a man in his 40s with a stressful job."

"And you found that reassuring?" Loren asked.

"What was reassuring was seeing my heart beating on a little TV monitor. Reassuring, and kind of creepy at the same time. When you consider how many things have to go right for us to stay alive, the only wonder is that any of us are here."

Loren made a head gesture that I interpreted as "Not in front of Elizabeth."

"Anyway, I'll get a professional to help me with my campaign. There are people who do this kind of thing all the time. It's what they do for a living. My job is just to show up where they tell me and look, you know, electable. And I may have to lean on Vivian a little more at work, but she can handle it. I've been training her to take over more all the time."

"You make it sound so easy, Norm," said Loren, "but something tells me that it's me who will have to take up the slack at home. But I'm not complaining," said Loren, holding up her hand as she complained. "If this is really what you want to do, then that's what we'll do. But will I have to show up at a bunch of political things with you? I really can't stand that stuff."

I wasn't feeling a great deal of support from my wife in this endeavor. Somehow I felt like Richard Nixon telling Pat he was running for president again in '68 after he'd promised her he wouldn't. I didn't like feeling like Nixon. I really didn't like thinking of Loren as Pat. Of course, Tricky Dick had won, hadn't he?

We closed out our meal of tortilla, beef and bean products and rolled ourselves out to the car, where I grunted as I bent over to strap Elizabeth in to her car seat like she was an astronaut preparing for launch. Within a couple of blocks of leaving the restaurant, Elizabeth conked out from her full belly, and she hadn't even had two margaritas like I had. I tried to draw Loren into more familiar ground by asking her about her day at work. Loren was well into her second decade working as a buyer for Neiman Marcus.

"It's just the same old, same old," Loren said. "It may still feel like summer outside, but we're well into getting the fall and winter lines in. Just peddling more expensive shit to people who don't need it, for higher prices than last year."

"Hm." I said. "I think you've just summed up the basis for the American economy. Think of yourself as a patriot on the front lines, defending our country from frugality. God knows, if you didn't sell high couture, don't think for a minute that the terrorists wouldn't."

As I began the unbuckling of Elizabeth from her safety contraption, she roused enough to open one eye and look at me. I heaved her out from the seat awkwardly, so as to avoid hitting her head on the roof of the car but to not miss one bit of the vertebra-stressing wrenching of my back.

"You're not getting any lighter," I said to my nearly-comatose daughter.

"Nope," she whispered in my ear, "I'm getting darker."

CHAPTER NINE

As I arose the next morning and prepared for work, I couldn't shake a dream I'd been having. If I dream every night, I'm not aware of it, but this one stood out to me for its un-dreamlike quality. The dream had felt more real than I felt running my electric shaver over my face and getting dressed.

And yet, at the same time, the details were slipping away with each slug of my coffee. I felt that the dream was important, and I didn't want to lose it, so I tried to review it as I made a selection from my tie rack. This was an automatic tie rack that, with a push of a button, turns round with a motorized whine to reveal each tie individually. This is the type of extravagance that tells one he has too much disposable income and should feel some first-world guilt. And I did feel guilty about the damn tie rack each morning that I pushed that stupid little button, but Loren and Elizabeth together had given it to me the previous Father's Day (from Neiman's, no doubt), so I felt obligated to use it. By the time your spouse "gives" you a new car for Christmas (like in the commercials, with a huge red bow tied around it, surely tied on by a domestic employee of some sort so as not to dirty one's own clothes by risking an oil stain from the driveway), it's too late to save your soul, so I still had some way to go.

Anyway, in the dream, I found myself in the modest little Methodist church which I'd attended as a child with my mother and sister. (If my father ever went there with us before he left the family, I don't remember). This church, when it had been built, was an outpost of Methodism on the suburban horizon of Branch Creek, just north of Dallas. My family was not particularly religious, but we did attend that little church religiously, at least until my older sister, and then I, finally made it clear to Mom that we didn't want to go anymore, and she gave up the Holy Ghost.

In the dream, though, I was in the church alone. There was no service in progress, and the chapel was empty. In fact, I got the distinct impression that I was really not supposed to be there, that I was, actually, holed up in the church like somebody in Montana making his last, long-bearded stance against the government. And I wasn't little Norm in the dream, I was an adult. The dream wasn't happening in my past. I was in the church, hunkered down, in the present. And I'd surrounded myself with familiar domestic objects. These objects were out of context and looked odd scattered around me on the stone and brick floor of the church: an alarm clock (the old fashioned, round kind with a big stem that you pushed in to set the alarm), a red toothbrush, a two-slice toaster, a broken Christmas decoration like the kind my Mom used to put on our tree. Things like that. There were others, but I don't remember them distinctly.

I had the impression that I'd been secreted in the church for a long time, when finally the main door opened, and in walked Mom and Erin, looking like they would have looked when I was kid in the 70s. Neither of them said anything, but one of them, maybe both, reached out her hand in the universal gesture that says, "I mean you no harm. Come with me. Let me help you." So I stood up, set down the clock that I'd been holding, and walked out of the church with them. No one was waiting for me outside, and I think I'd been looking for an expectant crowd that would either cheer or jeer my emergence. But there was no one, and I felt sad.

A dream like that is hard to shake off, but I kissed my wife goodbye and hugged my little girl as I headed for my car and the moving air pocket it would provide for my drive into Downtown Dallas. If either of them noticed any moodiness clinging to me, neither commented.

My cell phone rang as I was dancing my Volvo through the accelerate-and-brake traffic on Central Expressway. As I pressed the button on the phone's side to answer, I thought, not for the first time, will this be the day that I ram into a car in front of me while I talk on the phone instead of paying attention to where I'm going? This was idle musing, of course, because I would no sooner give up my cell phone than my car itself. Both were necessary accessories in my life.

It was Jeff calling.

"So how's the candidate today?" Jeff asked me. Actually, he sort of mumbled it, and he was hard to understand.

"Are you eating something?" I asked.

"Just a bagel. I'm heading into my office," Jeff said. I think he said that.

"Jeff, if you're eating a bagel and talking to me on your cell phone, what are using to steer your damn car with?"

"My knees, if you must know, counselor. But I just swallowed the last of the bagel, so I've got an extra hand for the steering wheel. Please don't turn me in, mom," Jeff said, more clearly now.

Jeff continued, "Hey, have you called Walter Stokely yet? The word's already out that you're running, so you need to call him."

"The word's already out?" I repeated. "Who...wait, one thing at a time. Who's Walter Stokely? The name's vaguely familiar, but I can't place it."

"Well, you'd better place it, man," said Jeff. "He's only the head of the Dallas County Democratic Party. If you want the party to back you, you need to call him before he hears about your candidacy from anyone else."

"Oh, right, I knew I'd heard the name. Fine, I'll give him a call when I get into the office. But who..."

"Hey," Jeff said, "I'm pulling into my parking garage, so we're gonna get..." and the call was dropped.

I soon pulled into my own underground parking garage, beeped my car locked as I walked away from it, and took the elevator to my 42nd floor office. I passed the desk of my secretary, Carol, on my way down the hall to my office, and she put her hand over the receiver into which she had been talking.

"Norm, are you really running for judge? When were you going to say something?" Carol had been with me for about nine years now, and she looked genuinely hurt.

I stopped for a moment and said, "Carol, this has just come up, I haven't had a chance to tell *anybody*. How did..."

"Wait a minute," Carol said, "I have to finish this call." She removed her hand from the receiver. "So, as I was saying, sir, you can set up an appointment to come in and see Mr. Spiczek..."

I decided to go on to my office rather than wait for Carol to finish.

Carol had already put two phone message slips on my desk before I arrived. One was from Samuel Avery, a client going through a divorce and trying to hide assets in the process. I had tried to convince him to reveal everything because the other side would find out anyway, and/or I would withdraw from his case if he lied on his sworn inventory and appraisement, and even if I didn't say why (something from which I would be prohibited by the rules of ethics), his wife's attorney would figure it out.

The other message was from Walter Stokely.

I buzzed Carol and asked her to call Mr. Avery back and see if she could get him into my office for an appointment without my having to speak with him first. The older I got, and the longer I practiced law, the more I found myself avoiding telephone conversations. When I had first begun practicing, and especially when I'd set out on my own as a solo practitioner, the sound of a ringing telephone made my heart beat a little faster and my adrenaline surge; clients were precious, and telephone time was billable time. A ringing telephone did the same thing now, but in a bad way. I had considered giving clients a break on their bills if they agreed to email all questions instead of calling me, but two of my advisors, Loren and Carol, counseled against it. I still think it would be a good idea, though.

Stokely, though, I would have to call, so I dialed his number and reclined in my high-back "executive" desk chair.

I asked for Walter Stokely and was in turn asked, imperiously I thought, who was calling. The receptionist's tone of voice was like the one I recall hearing in the *Wizard of Oz* when Dorothy and Co. were questioned at the door of the great castle in Oz who would dare approach and ask for the Great Wizard. Except when Dorothy said she was sent by the Good Witch of the North, the guard at the door changed his tune and said why didn't you say so in the first place? In my case, when I told the receptionist that I was returning Mr. Stokely's call (and it's possible that my tone was a bit imperious now, too), I received an actual sniff and the observation that I would have to wait while she saw if he was available to take calls.

I hoped Stokely was friendlier than his staff.

He wasn't.

"This is Mr. Walter Stokely."

He spoke as if he had no idea who was on the other end of the line, even though Roxanne the Receptionist must have told him. And who introduces himself as "Mister" anymore?

Well, I would try to muster a false enthusiasm anyway.

"Walter, Norm Spiczek here. I'm glad you called me this morning. I intended to call you as soon as I got in my office anyway, but you must be an earlier bird than me." That was fairly inane, but harmless, I thought.

"Ah, Mr. Spiczek. Yes, I have found that being early gives one an edge over the competition."

Stokely's voice was pitched high, possibly in an effeminate manner, or maybe just dilettantish.

"Hmm…," I responded. "So, what can I do for you?"

"Not much, I think. It's more a question of what I can do for you, Mr. Spiczek. I'm surprised that I didn't hear from you before you announced to the world that you intend to run for district judge as a Democrat in this town."

Truman Capote, I thought, that's who his voice reminded me of. Without the wit. More pugnacious.

"Oh, I'm sorry," I said, in my best sarcastic voice, "you weren't invited to my press conference? Oh, that's right, there was no press conference. Come to think of it, I haven't announced my candidacy to the world. I haven't announced it at all."

"Mr. Spiczek, perhaps we've gotten off on the wrong foot here," said Stokely. "My intention is to meet you, find out who this savior Democrat is who is riding to the rescue of the party but whom I've never met at any Democratic functions in the county. In other words, Mr. Spiczek, where have you been?"

"You can call me Norm, Walter. I've been practicing law in the Dallas County family law courts, is where I've been. That's what I've been doing for over 15 years now. And taking care of my wife and child. You could say I've been too busy to play politics, but now I've decided that I would like to run for family law judge. I've had a…a change of heart, and now I think this is what I'd like to do. Will that be okay with you, Walter?"

"Mr. Spiczek," responded Mr. Stokely, "you are free to do as you please, of course, following the changes in your body's organs as you see fit. It's just that there is a proper manner for doing these things. One is better served to work one's way up the ladder, as it were, rather than starting at the top. You know, pay your dues."

Now I was pissed.

"Walter, or Mr. Stokely I should say, I doubt the top of the ladder is family law district judge in Dallas County, unless we're talking about a stepladder, but the flattery is nice to hear. And I'm 42 years old, man, I don't have time to pay any dues. Still, though, it's nice to see that you have such a high opinion of an organization that has managed to get exactly one judicial candidate elected in this county in the last 20 years."

And this was true, if vicious. In 1996, a man who happened to share the same last name as a famous television talk show host won election to a county criminal court (one step below a district court) and served honorably for four years. At the next election, a Republican from the District Attorney's office ran against him, basing her entire campaign, as best I could see, on using billboards and flyers to point out that the judge was not the talk show host (e.g., "Miller Doesn't Talk the Talk or Walk the Walk. Don't be Fooled") and, more importantly, the judge was a *Democrat*, for God's sake. The prosecutor won in a landslide.

"I see," said Mr. Walter Stokely, sounding, improbably, more brittle than he had already. "Then perhaps we'll meet at a party function sometime, although someone will be required to point you out to me as I don't know what you look like. Good day, Mr. Spickzer," Stokely said, intentionally mispronouncing my name.

"Oh, you'll recognize me, Walter," I said. "I'll be the relaxed one without a rod up my ass." But I realized Stokely had already hung up.

How do these things happen, I wondered? I consider myself a pretty easy-going guy, nice to most people. Not effusive maybe, but I certainly hadn't expected to enter a war with the head of the party whose nomination I was seeking.

I did not shake my angry feeling as I tried to work on other projects that morning. In turn, I snapped at Carol when she said she couldn't find the "Rothschild" file I'd requested from her.

"Well, I doubt it just pushed the elevator button by itself and fled the building, Darlin'. Keep looking," I'd said. Shit does indeed flow downhill, and I saved "Darlin'" without a "g" for my testiest moments. It seemed LBJ-ish (the President, not the highway)."

I don't like being that way, though, and when Carol buzzed through just before lunchtime to tell me Jeff was holding on the line for me, I apologized for my earlier outburst.

"That's okay, Norm," said Carol, "I found the file about two minutes later, but I wasn't going to give it to you until I wasn't mad at you anymore. I'll bring it back in a few minutes."

"Oh, thanks," I said. I wonder if other lawyers face this sort of civil disobedience from their staff?

"Hey, Jeff, what's up?" I asked into the receiver as I continued to scan some unread emails on my computer screen, visually separating the wheat from the chaff, if I've got that agricultural reference correct.

"What the hell did you say to Stokely?" Jeff asked.

"Stokely? How did you know I even talked to Stokely? Do you have a bug on my phone, or what?"

Jeff made a tapping sound against his phone's receiver.

"*Hello?* Hello, Norman Spiczek, am I getting through?" Jeff said "This is politics, man. People will know everything you do from here on out. You can't take a shit in this town without people arguing about whether you used union-made toilet paper. Why the hell do you think the Democratic Party is so fucked up in this town, man? Did you think they would welcome you with open arms?"

"Well, sort of," I said. "I mean, I thought they'd be glad to have someone decent run for that bench. They could have gotten some political hack who was unqualified."

"Oh, Jesus, you are a babe in the woods, my friend, a fucking babe in the goddamned woods. Stokely *is* a political hack. That's who runs political parties. The really successful, functional people are out in the real world being, you know, successful and functional. They have better things to do than go to three party meetings a week attended by their same handful of political hack friends time after time. And if there's one thing political hacks like Stokely really don't like, it's an outsider like you coming in to run for office without having put in his time. It makes you look like the star quarterback in high school thinking the chess club should be honored that you dropped by."

"So," I said, "what you're saying is that none of this has anything to do with electing good people who will serve the community well?"

"Getting a qualified, electable candidate would be a happy coincidence," Jeff said, "not a result of good planning on their part. That's just the way it is."

"Then," I said, "what about this? What if I just blow off the party and do it my way? You know, run as a Democrat, but not really through the party? What about that?"

"Well, the problem with that is that you'll have a hard time finding an experienced campaign manager because none of them will want to piss off Stokely's crew. You need someone who knows the ropes and can guide you through the process, but these guys would like to be able to represent other Democrats in the future, you know, so it would be a risk for them to go with you."

"Oh," I said, "I've already thought about that. I want you to be my campaign manager, if you'll do it. I'll buy the beer."

There was a momentary silence on the phone line. Then, Jeff said, actually sounding a bit choked up, "I'd be honored to be your campaign manager, Norm. I may fuck it up, but I'd be honored."

CHAPTER TEN

Life can be so unpredictable.

On my way home after work, I was thinking of my upcoming dinner with Loren and Elizabeth because, on my way out the door in the morning, Loren had reminded me that we'd told Elizabeth we'd take her to "Gunnin' For Fun." This was the sort of franchise designed to make children deliriously happy and their parents simply delirious. For show, the place sold cardboard-tasting pizza and pink-icing covered cookies, crap like that, but its true reason for being was to stuff as many video games and digital, simulated killing machines into 5,000 square feet as possible.

Children, and a few pathetic teens and adults there without children, could shoot, stab, eviscerate and immolate any obstacle, be it human or be it superhuman with demonic power, in what seemed to be an endless variety of very loud and fiery ways. And all this for the price of a "Fun Gunnin'" card, which could be purchased by the overwhelmed parent in $25 increments but which then only read out the remaining balance on LED displays in "Fun Gunnin' Bullets" instead of American currency, all the better to keep you off balance until your credit card bill came in the mail many days later.

If the leaders of the former Soviet Union had been smarter, they would have spent their inflated defense budget on planting as many of these franchises in America as possible, instead of on nuclear warheads. When I stand in that place (and when you're in one, you can't tell whether you're in the Dallas, Atlanta, Phoenix, or Oklahoma City location because they're equally dim and hideous), it's hard to be optimistic about the future.

Even more difficult is seeing my precious little girl, her long, curly black hair pulled back in a pony tail, with her still perfect, unblemished skin, and cherubic smile, with her warm, puffy little hands gripped on the triggers of two automatic rifles, rat-tat-tatting at a target on the video screen in front of her. The twinkle in Elizabeth's eyes when she "hits" something with simulated bullets and makes it explode makes me sigh, but of course I can't be heard over the growl of the machine next to me whose evil villain keeps repeating, at jackhammer volume, "Enter And You Will Die! Enter And You Will Die!" I tell you, the place is a laugh riot.

It's no wonder to me that I read in the paper about children killing children and stuffing their bodies in drainage pipes; my only wonder is why it doesn't happen more often. Oh, and you can be all superior and ask why I would allow my little girl to go to such a place if it's so bad, but, you see, parents get outflanked on these things. A girl from Elizabeth's class had her birthday party at "Gunnin' For Fun" before we knew about the place, and Elizabeth came home aglow with the thrill of the hunt, talking about how it was the best time she'd ever had and could we please go back every night? Everybody was going there, and why couldn't she?

Loren and I took the tack of most parents when faced with this situation: diversion. Together, we can play the ol' shuffle and dance as well as any White House spokesman, at least for awhile. "Yeah, honey, 'Gunnin For Fun' sounds great, but do you know what's even better on a Tuesday night? This fish place on Henderson. They've got hush puppies like you wouldn't believe!" And this tactic worked, in the long run, about as well as it does with the White House press corps. And eventually, we grit our teeth and agree to go to the hellish place, like we had agreed to go tonight.

Except that when I arrived home and entered the house, everything was very quiet. Normally I would have heard Elizabeth chattering away about something, or at least Ingrid and Loren discussing the day in what served as their domestic business meeting each day after work, in which Ingrid would recount to Loren the excruciating details of the day's trials and tribulations, a recap that would include upcoming events at Elizabeth's Montessori school, potential playdates, and even the specifics of bowel movements (Elizabeth's, thank God, although I don't think anyone else's would be off limits to their discussion). But today, I neither heard nor saw anyone until I entered the kitchen and saw Loren going through the mail where it lay stacked up on the kitchen "island." (The idea that kitchens could have "islands" was not something of which I was aware until my adulthood; previously, I would have naively referred to such a thing as just more "counter." And, besides, if a slab of counter in the middle of the kitchen is to be an "island," is the balance of the counter space against the walls to be known as the "mainland?" And what of the tiled floor spanning the gulf? How far should we carry this geologic terminology thrust upon us by interior decorators? Sometimes I rebelled and simply told Loren she could find the scissors in the drawer under the counter in the middle of the kitchen. It is, thus, with small insurrections that we maintain our dignity in this absurd world).

"Hey," I said, entering the kitchen, "where is everybody? I thought we were paying a visit to hell tonight with Elizabeth."

Continuing to sort through the various envelopes and catalogs, putting most of them in the "throw-away" pile (but not before disposing of the non-recyclable clear-plastic-window envelopes first before putting the remaining paper in the recycle stack) Loren responded without looking up.

"I know I'm a terrible mother, but I asked Ingrid to take Elizabeth to that damn place herself. I told Ingrid I'd give her a bonus, and Elizabeth didn't seem to mind who took her as long she got to kill things. I would say I'm going to hell for not taking my own kid there like a good mother should, but that place *is* hell, so why check in early? And I just couldn't face it. I want to go out tonight, just the two of us, to a ridiculously expensive steak place where I may only get a salad. And a bottle of wine. What do you think?"

"Absolutely," I said.

I'm not completely stupid. I could see that my wife was in a fragile mood, and I was calculating my best approach to her. This was a delicate maneuver, akin, I think, to guiding a yacht into a boat slip without wrecking it. It took a deft touch, a skill honed through many years of marriage and not to be attempted by an amateur.

"I would be delighted," I said, "to be seen at one of Dallas' finest restaurants with one of Dallas' prettiest women." Now that was pretty good, I thought.

Loren made a quick sound like she was choking on a chicken bone. I think it was supposed to be a sarcastic laugh.

"I feel like a pig," she said. "I'm bloated, I have cramps, and I've had a terrible day. I wish I'd washed my hair his morning because it smells like old hay."

"Ah, you do know how to turn a man on, you she-devil!" I said.

I made my way around the corner to Loren's side of the island, intending to take her in my arms and kiss her. But Loren was quicker, having anticipated my move, and by gliding a step to her right, she stayed on her side of the island.

She put one hand out, palm forward.

"Don't touch me," Loren said. "I'm gross. Let me just freshen up, and then we'll go." I think I just ran the boat into the dock, but maybe I could still recover.

"Whatever you want, dear. You just take your time, and let me know when you're ready."

Nothing. Loren went on upstairs, and I could hear the water running in the sink from our bathroom. What she would do with water in the sink that would make her feel better fell into the ever-expanding category of "I just wouldn't understand," a category that grew over the years, admittedly, because I had given up trying to understand so very many things.

But while the Loren who descended the stairs five minutes later was no Mary Sunshine, she did appear to have a firmer grip on her hostility toward the world. I knew better than to approach her physically, so I simply opened the front door and ushered her out as if she were the queen and I was simply the royal doorman. I also knew better than to open Loren's car door for her; nothing pissed off Loren more when she was already edgy than excessive civility. She presumed it to be derisive, I think.

I approached our restaurant selection obliquely.

"Um," I asserted, "I don't suppose you'd want to go to Gustav's, would you?" This was a fairly expensive steak place with an excellent salad selection that seemed to fit Loren's earlier-stated requirements.

"Anything's fine," Loren said, to the windshield.

Now, admittedly, this is where I have a problem. Knowing when to leave it alone.

"Well," I said, "I doubt *anything's* fine. We could just go to McDonald's, but I'm guessing that wouldn't be fine. I think their salad bar lacks a certain…existence, I suppose you could say. That's why I mentioned Gustav's. It's a steak place that also has good salads. That's, you know, that's why I mentioned it."

Probably I was looking for some recognition from Loren of the consideration I'd put into my suggestion, some acknowledgement of my kindness and thoughtfulness.

Loren turned to look at me.

She said, "Well, I may have something more than a salad, maybe some chicken or fish. Gustav's is fine, if that's where you want to go."

"It's not where *I* want to go, I picked it with you in mind. I'll go wherever you want to go, dear, you just have to let me know. I can't read your mind, you know, and I'm not sure I'd like what it's saying now even if I could."

This same discussion in another part of town could have lead to a knife fight, but in our social circles, it lead only to figurative daggers thrown with eyes.

"I'm not asking you to read my mind. I said Gustav's is fine," Loren repeated to the windshield.

So, Gustav's it would be. There's nothing I enjoy more than choking down 16 ounces of expensive red meat in the company of a contentious woman. There would definitely be some wine involved.

Actually, though, Loren's mood lightened after we arrived at the restaurant, were seated and pampered by the waiter with the French accent (which was probably fake, by the way), and wine was poured. Loren got a filet and skipped the salad. She was on her second glass of wine when she asked me how my day had been.

"Interesting," I said.

I told Loren about how everyone seemed to know about my intention to run for judge before I'd even announced it, and then I told her about my disastrous telephone conversation with Walter Stokely.

"Is it important for you to get along with this Stokely guy?" Loren asked.

"Well, he *is* the head of the party in Dallas County. It couldn't hurt. But he's such a jerk. Evidently, he's much more concerned with how active you've been in the party than whether you're a good candidate or not. I just don't understand these people. It's not like Stokely has a track record of getting people elected. As far as I can tell, he's presided over the longest losing streak in Democratic history in this county."

Loren stabbed another piece of beef with her fork. Just before clamping her teeth into it, she said, "So ignore him."

I was flooded with love for this woman. Loren is my kindred soul who shares my view of the world and who supports me in all I do (when the chips are down). And I would have told her so except that the obsequious, fake French waiter chose that moment to interrupt us with the announcement that if we wanted to order soufflés for dessert, we should do so now as they required 20 to 25 "meenutes" of preparation time.

"No, no," I said, "we won't be getting any..."

"Chocolate," interrupted Loren. "I'll have a chocolate soufflé."

"Excellent selection, Madame," murmured Jacques, ignoring me completely as he backed away from the table with his head bowed. When did all this commentary from waitstaff on a customer's order begin? You can hardly go anywhere now without your waitperson saying, "Oh, great choice! That's my favorite!" Like I care. The day I need a waiter's approval of my order will be the day I stop eating out.

Returning to our broken dialogue, I said to Loren, "Yes, exactly. That's what I was thinking. I can do this without Stokely and the bullshit Democratic Party of Dallas. Besides, to win, I'll need a lot more votes than just from Democratic loyalists. I've got to get some crossover appeal. I've got to convince at least some Republican regulars that I'm not dangerous, that I won't remove children from their parents just because the kids are allowed to pray out loud. There has got to be a core of Republicans in this town who aren't all radical, right-wing nuts like Hildy Pierce. Oh, and Jeff is going to be my campaign manager."

At this, Loren raised her eyes to meet mine over the rim of her lifted wine glass.

"Has Jeff ever run a campaign before?" she asked.

"Well, no, but I've never been in one before, either, so we should be perfect for each other." I think I felt my synergy with Loren slipping. "I mean, do you think that's a problem? I could spend some money hiring a more-experienced campaign manager, but then I'd end up running the same old kind of campaign that keeps losing in this town. Really, when you think about it, what have I got to lose? The election, I guess, but I think I'd rather lose it my way than win it somebody else's way. I mean, I think. What do you think? I could hire a professional. Maybe I should."

Loren drained the last dregs of her wine glass, set it down, cleared a space in front of her on the table, and reached both of her hands toward me. I offered up my own hands to the softness and strength of her palms and fingers that I never failed to find arousing. In such ways are we reminded of the first flush of yearning we felt for these long-term lovers we call wives.

"Here's what I think, my love," Loren said. "This morning, when I went into Elizabeth's room to wake her up for school, I thought she was still sleeping when I sat on the bed beside her. But just before I put my hand on her shoulder, she let one eyelid barely open, and she said, 'You know, Mom, we all have wings. It's just that sometimes we forget how to use them.' So, Norman, use your wings."

CHAPTER ELEVEN

And I did fly into action. The first thing I did the next morning was to call Jeff and tell him we needed to get the word out about my candidacy, and we needed to do so for two reasons. First, I wanted to start nailing down support, both financial and name support, from as many prominent lawyers as I could. I wanted them for myself, and I wanted to make sure Hildy didn't get to them first. And I invited Jeff to lunch to begin discussing our campaign strategy.

I needed to make sure everyone at my office understood what I was doing, too, and that each of them knew their roles. So I called Carol and my associate, Vivian, into my office.

They sat down on the brown, leather couch next to each other, and I took one of the chairs opposite them.

"Before you hear about this from someone else, I wanted to be the first to tell you about my plans to run for judge of the 404th." Looking at Carol, I added, "However, it doesn't appear that I can stay ahead of the grapevine, so, in whatever order I may be, let me confirm that, yes, I am running for judge."

"Yeah," said Vivian, "Everyone knew by last night. And Hildy Pierce is running against you as the Republican. And Norm, just know that even though I normally vote Republican myself, you have my vote. I think you'll be a great judge."

"Oh," I said, "well, thanks, Vivian. I don't want you to go against your principles, but that's sweet."

Vivian had the rare combination of being overweight but not unattractive, in an overweight sort of way. The extra puffiness of her face removed worry lines and gave her the look of a teenager, though Vivian had just turned 30 about two months ago.

"What about you, Carol?" I asked. "Do you plan to actively campaign against me?"

"Not actively," said Carol. "I don't have the energy. Although if you become a judge, what happens to me, and to Vivian?"

"Well," I said, in an effort to buy time while I thought of an answer to this question I should have considered before now. "Obviously, I intend to make sure that both of you will be just fine. I haven't worked through all the details yet, but I would never leave either of you in the lurch. Besides, I probably won't win, anyway, so I doubt we have anything to worry about."

Carol looked at Vivian in a knowing way. Although technically Carol worked for both Vivian and myself, Carol's years of legal secretarial work caused Vivian to turn to Carol for practical advice on a daily basis. This put Carol in a mentor position to Vivian, and their union often left me on the outside looking in, sort of like at home with Loren and Ingrid. Wherever two or more women meet, a man is left out of the conversation.

Carol said, "What Norman means, Vivian, is that he just thought of this plan to run for judge, and he hasn't considered what it means for anyone other than himself yet. And I'm guessing, Norm," Carol said, glancing back at me, "that you haven't fully convinced Loren of the wisdom of this plan either, am I correct?"

"Well, no," I said, "but I think she's coming around. I mean, I don't think she fully understands it, but she's supportive. And maybe I haven't thought everything out yet, but I mean it when I say that I intend to do the right thing by both of you.

But really, it's way too early to start worrying about winning the election."

"Except," I added, "for one thing. I need signatures on petition sheets to get me on the ballot. A bunch of them, no later than January 2, although I would certainly want to get them sooner than that. Jeff Frankel will be my campaign manager and treasurer, so he'll help me with that, but it will probably require some social events and such to get people together to sign them. So, you know, I'll probably need some help with that. Of course, you don't have to do that; it's above and beyond the call of duty. If both of you could just hold things down here at..."

Vivian interrupted. "Jeff's going to be your campaign manager? Huh."

"What?" I asked.

"Nothing," Vivian answered. "I just thought that, you know, if you were serious about winning, you'd get someone with more..."

"Couth," finished Carol. "Aren't there professionals for this sort of thing?"

There are, I explained to Vivian and Carol, and they had a long track record of charging a lot of money and losing anyway.

"Look," I said, "if I'm going to lose this election, I'm going to lose it my way. What I don't want is to sit around on election night losing by 30,000 votes and wishing I hadn't played it so safe and conventionally. So I'm just going to say what I think and let it fly."

"From what I've heard around the courthouse," Vivian said, glancing at Carol for conformation, "you're well on your way. How important is the Democratic party to winning a race as a Democrat?"

So who the hell didn't already know about my argument with Stokely?

"Based on the election results I've seen," I said, "it's not that important, unless it narrows the margin of defeat. It's not the Democrats who concern me, it's the Republicans in this county. I've got to separate some of the Republican flock to have a chance."

"And your plan for that is to tell people who you really are and what you really think?" Carol asked in a skeptical tone of voice. "Norm, I've known you a long time, and some of your views and ways of dealing with things may not, you know, reassure some of the North Dallas blue-haired ladies, if you know what I mean."

Well nobody could accuse my informal cabinet of advisers of being shy with their opinions, but I liked the give and take (although there seemed to be more taking on my part than giving).

I pointed out to Vivian and Carol that the traditional Democratic candidates weren't winning the blue-haired lady vote anyway, so I had nothing to lose by doing things differently. By the time we finished our talk, both women had agreed to wholeheartedly campaign for me and be ready to pick up the slack that would be caused at the office by the redirection of my time and energy. Of course, I'd known they would come through.

As difficult as it was to do, I had to redirect my thoughts now to my law practice, as I had a meeting scheduled with a divorce client to talk about the strategy and goals for her case.

Gloria Stapleton was not my typical client, which was both good and bad. Gloria and her husband, Stephen, had been married for just over 20 years, and in that time had two children early in their marriage and had seen the youngest,

Bethany, off to college at The University of Texas last fall. Stephen had done quite well for himself working his way up in a large brokerage firm to vice president until, five years ago, he'd struck out on his own with a couple of his colleagues. Stephen had done even better with his own firm.

Stephen and Gloria had met while they were both in college, University of Texas students themselves, and Gloria was pregnant with their oldest, Mark, by the time she was a junior. With help from Gloria's parents and a lot of hard work in part-time jobs by Stephen, Gloria dropped out of college and raised, first, Mark, and then added Bethany later, while Mark went on to get his MBA. Gloria had stayed home to raise Mark and Bethany during their entire marriage, and by any measure of such things, she'd done a damn fine job of it. Both kids ended up with partial scholarships to UT, even though Stephen made enough money that he could have carried the whole load if he'd had to.

It was after Stephen went out on his own and had to hire his own staff that he'd begun his affair with his secretary, Maria. Sure, I could give you more of a build-up of how it happened, how Stephen resisted at first, how bad Maria felt about breaking up Stephen's good marriage (Maria had met Gloria and liked her), but what's the point? A boss having an affair with his secretary, with the out -of-town trysts and hurried phone calls in the driveway, the excuses for late nights at the office...well, what's new. In fact, the whole scenario is fairly pathetic in its unoriginality, and I found it, frankly, depressing in its familiarity.

But not as depressing as Gloria found it, to whom it was not a re-run but a just-released horror film. This is where Gloria was not the typical client. She wasn't angry, she wasn't looking for vengeance, she wasn't even startled at Stephen's behavior.

She knew she'd put on some weight over the years, hadn't paid attention to her body, hadn't developed new interests to keep her marriage to Stephen exciting. Her interests had been their children, and without their presence, Gloria's self-identity melted away to nothing in the period of a few months. She recognized that Maria was younger (but at least 34, as a mistress in her 20s might have been even harder to take), thinner, and Maria could talk endlessly to her husband about the business. Gloria didn't really care that much about Stephen's business, and she knew she should have taken more of an interest over the years. Maria had even gotten Stephen to take up tennis, something Gloria didn't have the slightest interest in doing.

This is what Gloria had told me, in a dull monotone, when I first discussed her case with her on the phone. She assumed, she told me, that Stephen would get most of the money they'd built up over the years (she wasn't even sure how much they had because Stephen, of course, kept up with all the "financial stuff"), that she'd have to find a job (doing what, she had no idea, having never received her degree and having not worked since a part-time job as a waitress at the time she met Stephen 20 years ago), and she just hoped she'd have some money for retirement. She didn't want to be too far away from her children in Austin, but she figured she probably would have to move in with her aging mother in her mother's Ft. Lauderdale condo. And mostly, Gloria didn't seem to care.

I asked Vivian to be present for my meeting with Gloria that was to take place in my office at 2:30. In preparation, I had asked Gloria to bring with her copies of her and Stephen's last three federal tax returns, which is something she was able to locate, surprisingly, in her husband's home office. Not only did I expect Vivian to handle many of the routine matters in

Gloria's case, thus allowing me to charge Vivian's lower hourly rate, I thought it was important in Vivian's young family law career to see how a client like Gloria is handled, or at least how I handled a client like Gloria.

Dealing with a depressed divorce client, as opposed to the more-common angry and vengeful one, carries its own risks and ethical considerations. There are some divorce lawyers who see it as their God-given mission to poke, prod, and punch their way into the most favorable result for their client, even if, or maybe especially if, their own client objects to such scorched-earth tactics. Then there is another class of lawyer who can't quit on a client fast enough, and having a client who willingly lays down on the tracks is a godsend for such a lawyer.

I have always tried to be a lawyer who never presses a client to do anything she doesn't want to do (it's kind of like sex in that sense), but I see it as my ethical duty to make sure the client understands all her options before she rules anything out. (Again, like sex). So, I will allow a client to give up before we ever start, but only if I'm convinced the client is mentally and emotionally sound enough to make such a decision rationally. And even then, I may cover my ass malpractice-wise by having the client sign a document agreeing that she has been advised of all her options and has chosen her course of her own free will. The divorce lawyer's nightmare, or at least one of several, is the client who swears she doesn't care about anything except finalizing the case and avoiding a trial, only to turn on her lawyer a few months down the line when the depression lifts.

At 2:30, Vivian and I walked up to my office suite's conference room, with its table that seats eight and floor-to-ceiling windows that offered a view of Downtown Dallas and north from a 42nd floor perspective, and met Gloria Stapleton.

I hadn't expected Gloria to be as attractive as she was. It's not that she was a knockout, but she was...well, oddly enough, the phrase that came to my mind was "efficiently pretty." I found the phrase odd because I'd neither heard it nor used it before, but it fit this woman exactly. She had shortish, black hair that betrayed no gray. If I had been more naïve, I might not have realized that Gloria dyed her hair to keep it that black, but with my own black hair getting increasingly white at its peripheries, and knowing Gloria was about my age, I could figure out the chemistry. It was the kind of thick but tightly-packed hair that is long enough to swing easily with the movement of Gloria's head but not take too long to wash and dry. Dororthy Hamill had made the look popular when Gloria and I were both teenagers.

She also was...well, here I go again, well built. This term is normally applied to a man, but Gloria was solid, in a pleasing way. Sure, her rear end was certainly broader than it must have been 20 years ago (and almost certainly broader than that of Stephen's new girlfriend), but it wasn't bad. And in the battle between gut and breasts, Gloria's breasts still had the lead. Funny thing was, though, I knew that what I found pleasant about Gloria would not be enough to keep a man sexually attracted after so many years. She just didn't have the kind of looks that would keep a roaming eye still, but many men would be delighted to take her home and would enjoy making her happy. And by the way, being a man, I made the foregoing analysis in the time it took for me to walk around the conference table to shake Gloria's hand as she stood up to shake mine. Perhaps this is what we have been left to do with the primordial instincts that formerly were used to size up a charging rhinoceros. It's quite a comedown, yes, but useful in our modern jungle.

After introducing the two women, I motioned for Gloria to resume her seat. She looked momentarily hesitant, as if her body was saying, "Sit, stand, collapse into a heap on the floor, whatever. What difference does any of it make, anyway?" But Gloria did sit.

Just to verify that I had Gloria's account of her marriage and impending divorce correct, I had her hit the highlights for Vivian, while Vivian earnestly took notes on her yellow legal pad. (These "legal" pads, by the way, are all now "letter" size, not "legal" size, as they once were. Not even lawyers use "legal" size paper any more, so calling a "letter" size pad a "legal" pad is one of those ghost phrases I've been collecting in my head for some time. Like "roll up the car window" when what is really meant is "push that button in a certain way that causes the window to close." Or "carbon copy." Et cetera.).

Gloria recounted her marriage to Stephen with all the enthusiasm one might expect from a tour guide at Monticello reciting the same facts, dates, and descriptions for the 5,000th time. But I don't think Gloria's dullness resulted from repetition; Gloria was just dull. My mother would say Gloria had a "flat affect." I had thought that was a fussy-sounding phrase, but I saw with Gloria that it had its place.

When Gloria ran out of words, or the energy to utter any more, I asked her, "So the question now is, 'what do we do?'"

Gloria looked at me without enthusiasm and said, "You know, I really don't care. I just want this divorce over with. If Stephen wants his new life, let him have it. He got everything I had to give for 20 years, and now I'm just tired."

"Gloria," I said, as Vivian looked from the client to me, "I'm going to ask you to do something that won't be easy. When someone is in your position, it's very hard to see past tomorrow. It just seems to take all your energy to get from one moment to the next. Does that sound accurate?"

Gloria nodded.

"Well," I said, "I want you to really concentrate on something. If you can, imagine where you want to be five years from now. I'm not promising I can get you there, but I know that without a plan, it's very easy to just drift, sometimes for years. You've got too much life left to live to do that, and if you'll tell me what you really want, maybe I can help you get it."

I stopped talking, and Gloria looked down at her folded hands resting in her lap. She sighed.

"I guess I'll have to get a job and a place to live. I have to survive, somehow. I'll probably become one of those apartment people."

"Apartment people?" I asked.

"You know," said Gloria, "those poor people who live in apartments." Sigh.

Good God, I could never allow this woman to see the inside of a courtroom.

And with that, incrementally, Gloria focused on what she needed, and wanted, for her future. As she did so, her vibrancy picked up, ever so slowly. Energetic? No. But at least she was stringing together a couple of sentences at a time, and with a furrowed brow was creating the rough draft of a plan.

I even got her to chuckle when I said, "Now, Gloria, unless you have a couple of boyfriends on the side and you want to marry one of them right away, you should really be in no hurry to get this divorce. In fact, time is on your side. It's Stephen who's probably in a hurry. So we're going to test just how quickly and how badly he wants this divorce. The first thing we'll do is get some temporary orders in place that force Stephen to pay your household expenses and provide you with some temporary spousal support. I'll try to make those orders open-ended, so Stephen can think about paying you monthly for a long time. Then, when we think Stephen is really ready to settle, we'll get this case to mediation, and we'll take a hard-line stance that he must pay you alimony for quite some time and agree to give you more than half of the community estate. I will also start digging into his business, which should serve to make him a bit antsy. Let me handle the nasty stuff, and if he gives you a hard time, you just tell him it's your lawyer's fault."

So, had I pushed Gloria into putting up more of a fight than she wanted to? Yes, probably. Was it the right thing to do? I have no idea, but it felt right.

CHAPTER TWELVE

We all are steeped in astounding ignorance about the world around us. From what I can see, we cope by either ignoring our ignorance (which itself requires some astounding mental exercise) or by imagining a simple-minded explanation for unexplainable phenomena and then refusing to examine the questions again.

For example, the vast majority of human beings get up each day, get dressed, go to work, eat, come home, love, play, entertain ourselves, knowing, but not believing, that we *will* die. We will cease to exist. It's a certainty. Every single human being alive today lives each moment under a death sentence, the terms and conditions of which are unknown to us and from which there is no hope of a reprieve from the Governor. Talk about "cruel and unusual."

Except that it isn't unusual, it's just "life." Or "death." They amount to the same thing. It really doesn't do to look too closely at this "death" thing, I believe, but, when I do open that door on occasional sleepless nights, and just before I slam it closed again, I think, "Good God, am I the only one who thinks this is bizarre?" Well, given humankind's preoccupation with religious explanations of life and death, clearly I'm not, but still…death is bizarre.

But you don't have to think about life and death itself to realize that we're drowning in an ocean of ignorance. I know that airplanes work, but I don't know how. So many of us, including myself, think we're so smart, but if I were time-warped to the 13th Century, could I explain how an airplane works in convincing detail? Could I build a demonstration model? Of course not. Oh, sure, I know about "thrust and lift" and all that, but so did a lot of people before the Wright Brothers, and they couldn't build airplanes either.

If you want to know how unaware you are of the world in which you live, just wait until your four-year-old daughter asks you "How come when you plug in a cord, the lamp comes on?" And don't think you'll get away with saying, "Because, dear, that's where the electricity comes from."

Maybe this is what drives the unquenchable thirst in our society today to be famous, or at least to be known. We're surrounded by so many unexplainable forces that seem, and are, so much bigger than any individual, that we're scared we'll die without leaving any impression on the world. And, of course, we will, no matter who we are or how famous we were in life. Hey, that's "life." And "death." Any of our tombstones could aptly read, "Here lies [fill in the blank]. Known by some, unknown by most."

This is what I was thinking when I looked at a questionnaire from the Dallas paper that they had sent to all the candidates for judicial and political races in the county. There was a series of questions about each candidate's personal and political histories and beliefs, and the final question was: "Why did you decide to run for this office/bench?"

I squelched my first response ("Shit if I know"), and reconsidered my second choice ("Because I almost hit a parked van on the way home from playing golf"). Nope. ("I refuse to lead a life of quiet desperation" didn't hit the right note either). So, I wrote something along the lines of how I wanted to give back to the profession and the community that had given me so much in my life, or some such crap.

But why, really, was I doing this? Ego, of course, the same thing that drives every politician, and that's not all bad, either. More specifically, though, I wanted to be remembered. Next time I came upon a parked vehicle at full speed, and I wasn't lucky enough to miss it, I wanted there to be an article in the newspaper about my life and death, even if it was in the back of the Metro section.

But no, that wasn't all of it. The fact is, I hadn't paid enough attention to politics and the political world around me while I had been busy building a practice, enjoying my marriage to Loren, and then being a father to Elizabeth. Maybe now that Elizabeth was getting older, I was paying more attention to the direction of my city, state and country, and I didn't like what I saw. I found myself talking out loud to the newspaper in the morning, saying things like "What a moron," or "You've got to be kidding." Loren would raise her eyebrow as she walked past the breakfast table and hear me, and one time Elizabeth asked what a "moron" was, so I tried to cool it. But I was agitated.

Aren't we all trying to impose a narrative on our lives, which are really a series of unconnected, happenstance events? Sort of like dreams. In dreams, our synapses fire out a bunch of individual scenes, and our brains work furiously to connect the dots. Maybe we're doing just that whether we're asleep or awake, whatever "awake" means.

Anyway, I completed the questionnaire and mailed it off.

The first confrontation of the election (if you didn't count my phone conversation with Walter Stokely) was due to take place in a few weeks. Three months had passed since I first decided to run for judge, and in that three months, with Jeff's loyal help, I had managed to get the necessary signatures on a petition to place myself on the ballot as the Democratic nominee (there was no other Democrat running for the 404th, so there would be no primary fight) and pay my filing fee. Getting signatures I could understand, but having to pay money to get on a ballot seemed un-American to me. Evidently, I had a lot to learn about the reality of American electoral politics, even at the local judicial level.

The forum would be our very own Bar group of Dallas, in the old building that had been updated and expanded to accommodate this town's ever-growing population of lawyers. The multiple additions and updates to the former private mansion over the years proved that lawyers love to talk, and they don't mind talking to each other, if no one else will listen. And they want a nice-looking place with tuxedoed waitstaff in which to hold these conversations, or mutual monologues as they so often were, so after a few million dollars and the lure of having your firm name put on a brick in the walkway, they got it. Yes, my name was there with all the rest, but I'd been so outspent by others that my brick was halfway down the parking garage ramp, in the perpetual darkness between the daylight from the street and the lights from deeper into the garage. I knew it was there because I'd gotten out of my car and searched for it one night with my headlights on, and I thought of it every time I drove over it.

The agenda was that, while the Family Law Section of the Dallas Bar ate its way through salads and overpriced lasagna, my opponent and I would each have a few minutes to expound on our qualifications for the bench. I'd been to these sorts of things before, and they were generally quite boring, with both judicial candidates looking uncomfortable and affronted by the indignity of campaigning for a judicial office, but this is what our state makes us do, so we do it. Never had I seen a judicial candidate speak directly to his or her opponent or even acknowledge the existence of an opponent, and there was no reason to think that this event would be any different.

The rumors of Hildegard Pierce running as the Republican candidate had, of course, turned out to be true because, as maddening as the courthouse grapevine is, one thing it usually isn't is wrong. If only the President had possessed such accurate intelligence before he took this country to war. All he would have had to do was send an advance squadron of lawyers into Iraq, given them about a week, and they could have told him everything he needed to know. Sure, some of the weaker among the pack may have been lost along the way, but the real survivors would have emerged with lots of billable hours and plenty of arguments. Talk about weapons of mass destruction.

To prepare for this foray into the "public" (if an incestuously-familiar group of fellow family lawyers could be called the public), Jeff suggested that he and I play golf the day before. Here's how he made his suggestion, on the phone.

"Hey, you need to get your ass out of the office tomorrow and play some golf with me so we can get you ready for the candidates' forum."

"I've got a client meeting at 2:00 in the afternoon," I said.

"Cancel it. The election comes first," Jeff responded.

"Yeah," I said, "but you aren't talking about the election, you're talking about golf."

"This is *business* golf," Jeff said, the sound of traffic in the background. "You can use the campaign donations you receive to repay yourself for it later. And we need to go to a really nice course, for inspiration."

Reflexively, I ran my hand over my forehead. My forehead has been expanding lately. I can pretty much fit the span of my hand, if I keep my thumb and fingers together, between my eyebrows and my hairline. This was not always so. Well, not my whole hand, but I think that, at this rate, I'll be able to fit the whole hand in by this time next year. Most people think these things are gradual, but I'm fairly certain my forehead expansion could be traced to the birth of my daughter, almost five years ago. It was a Thursday, around 5:30 in the afternoon.

"What?" I said into the phone.

"I said," said Jeff, speaking loudly, "I'll get us a tee time at the Cowboys' Club."

The Dallas Cowboys (read: Jerry Jones) built a golf course near DFW airport that has quickly become one of the premier courses in the area. Each tee box has a marker that looks like a headstone, commemorating an important event in Cowboys' history, including the purchase of the team by Jerry. Given the lack of success with which the team has plagued the Cowboys-besotted city since the late 90s, the "headstone" metaphor has taken on added resonance. Come to think of it, the fall of the team more or less coincided with the erection of this golf monument to Jerry Jones, which could be some proof of God's existence. It was like a "smiting" and was kind of reassuring, when you thought about it.

Jeff interrupted my musing again.

"Goddamn it! Pick a fucking lane and stay in it, dickhead! Not you, Norm, it's this asshole in front of me," Jeff said.

"Naturally," I replied. "You never see the assholes behind you."

"What?" said Jeff.

"Never mind. Where are you, anyway?"

"On LBJ," Jeff replied, "getting nowhere, fast."

"Hmm...Look, I'll get Vivian to cover the client conference tomorrow. I'll probably lose the business, but I guess I'd better get used to it," I said. "I have a feeling there'll be a bunch more of these kinds of conflicts before the election."

"That goddamn name: 'Vivian,'" Jeff said. "It always

reminds me of 'vivisection.' I don't even know what a 'vivisection' is, but it sounds nasty. I mean, I like Vivian, the person not the name, just fine, it's just..."

"I'll see you on the golf course tomorrow, Mr. Frankel," I said, and hung up.

When I told Vivian she would need to cover the client conference, she said she would be glad to but that the client wouldn't like it. This was followed by Carol putting through a call to me from Loren that Elizabeth was home early from her Montessori School for the Training of Young Vegans (my pet name) because of a fever. It was Ingrid who had called Loren to tell her about Elizabeth. I'm at the end of the chain. We never sat down and developed a flow chart for this relay of information concerning my daughter, but it was understood. At least, it was understood by Ingrid and Loren, and probably Elizabeth, my daughter's Montessori "guides" and maybe even Carol, but I'm not sure I understood it. On the other hand, I must admit that I didn't question it either. I remember from law school that my response would be called "ratification." Someone without proper legal education might call it "capitulation," but what do they know?

After maneuvering my way home down the stop and go traffic of Central Expressway (which, to be more precise, was more "drive like hell for 200 yards, then slam on the brakes, see an opening, scream forward, slam on the brakes, wait for another opening," etc.), I exited in University Park, my own little up-scale, exclusive hideaway of a town sitting in the middle of North Dallas like the Red Spot on Jupiter. If anyone tried to take up this prime land from the City of Dallas today and create the "Park Cites," it would never be allowed. But The Bubble, as those both inside and out of the Park Cities called the area, was created when North Dallas was just scrubby farmland in which most people didn't see a future. There's certainly nothing topographically interesting about the place, but like that experiment with the biosphere in Arizona or wherever, The Bubble has created its own environment over the years. Here, the houses that were torn down to make way for bigger houses are themselves torn down to make way for even bigger houses. And, I maintain, no matter how hot it is in Dallas, when I turn off Central Expressway and drive past the University Park city limits signs, the read-out on my car thermometer always drops a degree or two. It's weird.

I do carry a certain amount of guilt for living in UP, as a Democrat and all. If I were to ever doubt the Republican, far-right political leanings of my neighbors, all I need do is observe the yard signs that bloom like bluebonnets every election season. And that's what they're like: wildflowers. You know how you can look out from a Texas highway in the spring and see nothing but an ocean of bright colors? The closer it gets to November around here, you see an ocean of the same-colored yard signs, usually occupying a very narrow bandwidth of hues along the red, white, and blue spectrum. And then, occasionally, like recalcitrant weeds among the eye candy, you'll see a sign for a Democrat, at least until that sign is eradicated in the night by a pest controller (which may be the UP police themselves, for all I know, protecting the hosts of such weeds from their own folly, in the interests of preventing riots, which would be catered affairs, of course). My yard sprouts such weeds in election years. The blight has been noted, and Loren and I don't get invited to so many "block parties" any more.

Well, to hell with it anyway, the schools here are good, and we plan to send Elizabeth to the local elementary school when she's of age, and the neighborhood is safe and secure. Property values are great and ever-rising. And it's at least two degrees cooler here than in the City of Dallas. If I sound defensive, it's because I am. I foresee future battles with Elizabeth's teachers over the curriculum, where they will constantly try to sneak in positive references to Ronald Reagan and publicly pray about stuff, but maybe I'm just paranoid. (Like most paranoid people, though, I don't think I am).

I click open the rolling gate from the alley leading into my driveway and click it shut again behind me. When I enter the house, I see my daughter on the couch watching Disney on TV. (Disney unnerves me, but I won't get into that now). Elizabeth heard me come in, and she leans back on the arm of the couch, letting her waterfall of curly black hair cascade from her head, actually puts the back of her right hand lightly upon her forehead, and whispers to me, "Father, have you heard that I'm ill?"

Loren and I have both accused each other over the years of Elizabeth's life of inculcating our daughter with Victorian novels, but we each deny it. I know *I'm* not the one who has taught Elizabeth to speak or act in such dramatic fashion, but here lies Emily or Charlotte Bronte (I could never tell them apart) in my living room, apparently having a fainting spell. This is not uncommon behavior for Elizabeth, but it's always a jolt to me.

To complete the picture, Elizabeth is wearing the most old-fashioned, long nightgown she owns, white with little flowers on it, so that if it weren't for the television blaring out the voice of a dormant celebrity mouthing the words of a cartoon character, this scene could have taken place in Dorset in 1862. Without knowing, I feel that not everyone's life is like this.

"Yes, my daughter," I say as I kneel down beside her, "word of your malady has spread far and wide. How be you now?"

I saw my goal accomplished when Elizabeth smiled,

slightly, and said to me, "Daddy, why are you talking so funny?"

Loren came in, and when I mentioned to her that Elizabeth seemed to be feeling better, Loren dismissed my diagnosis like so much background chatter.

"101.4" I think this was Elizabeth's temperature, not the radio station my wife wanted me to listen to.

Loren's declaration called for a response, so I asked when that temperature reading had been taken. It was understood, though, that I was merely between spouses of a certain tenure, that I was merely falling back on ingrained legal training to ask a question in a situation where you know a response is called for, but you have not yet worked out that response. Loren didn't answer.

I went upstairs to change clothes while Loren and Ingrid consulted about Elizabeth's condition. Women do this sort of thing to reach emotional equilibrium rather than to convey information; after all, both of the women in my house knew Elizabeth's temperature, and they knew without discussing it that the proper course of treatment was alternating ibuprofen and acetaminophen to bring the fever down, and if Elizabeth didn't improve within 24 hours, we'd take her to her pediatrician. (At least, I think that's the proper procedure, from overhearing previous consultations between Ingrid and Loren on the same subject).

When I came back downstairs, Elizabeth called to me from the couch.

"Daddy, Mommy said you're going to tell people what to do."

I must have looked puzzled because Ingrid, who had been standing nearby, explained to me that what Elizabeth meant was that Loren had told Elizabeth about my plans to run for judge. Is that how Loren saw my quest, as just a bid to make people do what I told them to do?

"Is Mommy a judge, too?" asked my insightful child.

If that's the definition, then yes, I thought, not so charitably, or fairly. The key to a good marriage or to being a good parent, though, is not so much what you say as what you don't say, and I didn't say what I had just thought. Instead I described, in five-year-old terms, what a judge does in a family law court. Elizabeth lost interest, though, somewhere between "divorces" and "conservatorship proceedings." I need to pep up that description, I thought.

I must give Elizabeth credit for forcing me to think harder, more deeply, about my running for judge. At dinner, where my Victorian daughter sat cross-legged in a chair with two blankets pulled up to her neck and just the right pallor to her face, emphasized by her dark black hair, Elizabeth asked me, apropos of nothing in the conversation we'd been having, "So why *do* you want to be a judge, Daddy?"

Kids ask the darnedest things, right? Or maybe their questions aren't so unusual, but when those questions are asked by a child, answering them becomes more difficult. The struggle between elucidation and evasiveness is more prominently in the mind of the adult who must answer. Not to mention that the audience for my answer included Loren, who I could tell was eager to hear my answer.

"Well, honey," I began, "it's really very simple. I...I think I can help people, you know, I can make a difference in their lives." Elizabeth stared back at me, visibly losing interest in my answer. "I think I'd be a good judge, and I feel like this is what I want to do with my life right now."

And that was it. I'd stumbled onto the answer, but once I said it, it rang true.

Elizabeth went back to pushing a couple of peas around on her plate, one at a time, creating her own organic version of the "dot race" shown at ball games on the Jumbotron. She did add, however, "I think you'd be a good judger, too."

And Loren said, smiling, "I think you're right, honey. Daddy would be a good judger." Thus, my little girl helped me explain my quixotic pursuit and finally aligned Mommy with Daddy's desire. Was it the ibuprofen or the acetaminophen, or something else, I should thank?

CHAPTER THIRTEEN

Y ou know what you never see?" Jeff asked me on the golf course the next day, as he drove and I walked from the first green, which I'd bogeyed by missing my three-foot putt, and Jeff had parred.

"A good putt?" I asked.

"Baby squirrels," Jeff said. "You see squirrels all the time, but where are the tiny little baby squirrels? They must have babies, but you never see them."

"Hmm. I guess not. And what about dead birds," I said. "I mean, you see dead birds sometimes, but it's unusual enough that you notice. We're surrounded by birds all the time, and they have to be dying, so you'd think we'd see a lot more dead birds than we do."

"Of course," Jeff responded, as he pulled his driver out of his bag on the second tee with a grunt, "the birds might be wondering the same thing. You know, like (and here Jeff does an odd impression of how a bird might talk on the golf course, if birds talked, which I think he got from some cartoon), 'you know what you never see? Dead humans. We're surrounded by humans, but you rarely see a dead one.' It's because we're in funeral homes, you know, where the birds can't see us, except for murder victims who are dumped at the lake."

Jeff, after one quick practice swing, launches a perfect drive down the right side of the fairway that draws nicely into the middle, where it lands and bounces forward another 30 yards or so. Now it's my turn.

As I take the cover off my driver, I say, "You do this just to fuck with my concentration, don't you?" Jeff shrugs.

My drive also starts out right and comes left, but smack into the center of a mesquite tree, which rejects the golf ball like a bad transplant and spits it back 20 yards toward where I stand on the tee box, watching my ball return when all I'd wanted was to send it far on its way toward the next green. As a golfer, I believe the tree has acted with malice.

I've never felt at one with nature. Occasionally, I feel that nature and I have come to an understanding, but the feeling is fleeting. I respect nature, and I try not to get in its way, but we've never seen eye to eye.

As I walk down the fairway to my ball, and get to it far too quickly, Jeff drives beside me in his cart. His first beer, a "diet" one, sits in the cup holder built into the cart. Jeff hasn't popped the top on it yet, adhering to some internal regulation he has for when he's allowed to begin drinking. Jeff chooses the moment in which I approach my ball to begin speaking about the election.

"So I've been thinking about your election strategy, and what I think is that you should just be yourself," Jeff said.

I had been taking a practice swing while Jeff spoke. Still holding my club in the air in my imaginary perfect follow-through (which I would never repeat when I swung the club for real), I stopped my body's motion and turned my head to Jeff.

"That's it? That's your strategy? Be myself? How long did you think about that? Am I paying you for this?"

Jeff reached for his beer and popped the top.

"No, and don't get pissy about it. I'm just saying, don't try to be all 'politcally-correct' and shit. Just say what you think and let the chips fall where they may," Jeff said. He took a long swig from his beer, and then wiped his mouth on his shoulder. "You know, don't try to be so careful."

I shook my head, rolled my eyes, and swung at the ball. My 3-wood made such solid contact that I felt that feeling that's no feeling at all. It's that feeling you feel when you hit a ball, whether it's a golf ball, a baseball, or a tennis ball with such perfect balance and control, that the club/bat/racket is nothing but an extension of your arm, and you don't even feel the contact. It's the second-best feeling a man can feel, and as he gets older, it may take the lead, if you know what I mean. The ball shot straight down the fairway, and if my drive hadn't been so bad, it would have made it all the way to the green. As it was, the ball rolled to a gentle stop about fifteen yards in front of the green, smack dab in the middle of the fairway.

"Yeah," said Jeff, *"that's* what I'm talking about. Grip it and rip it."

I couldn't wipe the grin off my face.

"Are you talking about golf or the election?" I asked.

"Yes," Jeff responded.

I continued to play well as Jeff and I made our way around the course. I was thinking about election strategy more than golf, and Jeff did get a bit more specific with his ideas as we played.

"See," Jeff expounded after easily dropping his golf ball onto another green in regulation, "Hildy Pierce is a conservative in every way, not just in politics. I had a case with her once where I'd been appointed by the court to represent some crack-head parents where the state had removed their two kids. I mean, yes, my people were absolute trash, but they did love their kids. Hildy went for termination of parental rights, even though the parents kept overcoming every obstacle that CPS could put in their way: drug tests, parenting classes, counseling, the whole gamut. But none of that mattered to Madame Prosecutrix because she was out for blood. Hell, even Child Protective Services, her own client, told her, in front of me, that they'd be willing to give these former crack-heads another chance, with strict supervision. But Hildy forced the damn thing to trial, and I'll never forget what she told me before the case was called in front of Judge Simmons."

Here Jeff put his hand on his hips and mocked Hildegard Pierce's stern, humorless voice. (Jeff was into impressions today, from birds to the bird-brained). " 'These people have sinned, counselor, and now they must be punished.'"

"Jesus," I said, as I lined up my shot from the fairway, calculating my best approach to the elusive green. "What did you say to that?"

"I said," Jeff remembered, "I don't recall seeing that language in the Texas Family Code.

I was about to speak again, but decided to hit first, so without any practice swing, I simply swung my 5-iron and arced a magnificent shot that plopped down onto the front of the green and rolled forward, to what turned out to be about five feet or so from the pin. My ball was at least ten feet closer to the hole that Jeff's.

We both stared at my shot in disbelief, but I didn't want to drop the thread of Jeff's story.

As I returned my club to the bag and started walking toward the green, and Jeff punched the accelerator on his cart, I asked, "So what happened in the trial?"

Matter of factly, Jeff said, "I kicked her ass. In fact, Simmons, in so many words, asked why the hell Pierce was wasting his time with this case when she had more important stuff to hear."

"What did Hildy do?"

"Oh," said Jeff, taking another swig of weight-losing beer, "I'll never forget this part, and this is what I'm trying to tell you. I didn't say a word to her after we were finished, but she made a point to walk over to my side of the counsel table and say, 'You may have won here today, Mr. Frankel, but there is a higher court judging all of us, and you should pray that you'll do as well there.'"

"You're kidding," I said. "She really said that?"

"Absolutely," said Jeff. "And my telling her to go to hell probably didn't improve our personal relationship any."

"No," I said, "I can see how somebody might take that the wrong way."

We'd made our way to the green, where Jeff took one quick look from his ball to the hole, from which I'd removed the flag, and gently and with perfect rhythm propelled his ball on a laser course for it. As his ball slowed down, though, about three inches from its target, it barely curled off to the right and came to a stop right beside the hole.

"Shit," Jeff said, "I misread it."

I lined up my own putt, stood behind it, knelt down for a better view, stood over it, took a couple of practice swings, took a deep breath and exhaled to relieve tension, just as I'd read in a golf magazine, and stroked the ball with my putter. The ball rolled nicely, slowed down just in front of the cup, and barely fell into the front of the hole.

"Good God," I said, "a par. I never beat you on this hole."

"You're learning," Jeff said, grunting as he bent down to pick up his golf ball. "But this is only the 11th hole. You haven't won yet."

CHAPTER FOURTEEN

I 've never liked these things," Stanley Canon said to me as we stood in line at the buffet table in the converted mansion that serves as the headquarters for the Dallas Bar Association.

"Overcooked, rubbery chicken breasts? What's not to like?" I asked, checking out the usual selection of unimaginative offerings from the industrial kitchen located in some part of the building to which lawyers are prevented from entering. I'm sure the staff is concerned about lawsuits. Putting the food out on the tables at 11:00 for a noon Family Law Section meeting and letting it harden under the heat lamps for an hour did nothing to increase its palatability.

"No, no," said Stanley, "these Section meetings. Particularly these meetings where we have a candidates' forum." Stanley had been a family lawyer a little bit longer than me, which means too long. "I mean, no offense, Norm, but the candidates never have anything interesting to say, and most people in that room already know who they're gonna vote for before you ever speak. The whole exercise is just a waste of time. Oh, and you're right, the food sucks, too."

"Well, thanks for the pep talk, Stanley, but I have to get up there on the dais now and hope I don't spill any food on myself while I eat in front of 200 colleagues. Believe me, the candidates' forum is no joy for the candidates, either. No one cares what you have to say if you do show up, but if you don't show up, the lawyers feel slighted. So, what the hell, we all just go through the routines."

Balancing my salad bowl and lunch plate, I entered the wide double doors to the meeting room. The round tables for 10 toward the back of the ballroom were filling up quickly, allowing an unobtrusive and quick exit for those lucky enough to snag such a prime position. The tables near the front were becoming occupied more reluctantly, except for a handful of squirrelly lawyers, mostly newer ones, who still thought they were in school and would get "extra credit" for sitting toward the front. I knew, as did most of the lawyers in the room, that we came here each month because it was a cheap and easy way to gain Continuing Legal Education credits, of which every active lawyer in Texas must have a minimum of 15 hours each year to remain in good standing with the state bar. How listening to two judicial candidates talk about themselves for a few minutes each would constitute "continuing legal education" was anybody's guess, but I doubt many complaints would be heard from the crowd, despite Stanley Canon's critique. Lawyers always enjoy a good conflict, and it beats the hell out of listening to another accountant explain the federal child tax deduction for the umpteenth time.

As I wound my way through the tables and toward the raised dais, I saw that Hildy Pierce was already seated and primly nibbling on her lettuce. As best I could tell, lettuce was all she had on her plate. She was dressed in a conservative blue business suit with a white ruffled blouse under her jacket, buttoned up to her neck lest anyone suspect she sported a pair of breasts. Evidently, Hildy had adopted her style of dress in the 80s, and if it was good enough then, by damn, it was good enough now.

She looked so timid and nervous taking little bites of salad and quickly scanning the room that I almost felt sorry for her. It must be difficult for a shy, businesslike person like Hildegarde

Pierce to stand up in front of her colleagues and brag about herself. Sure, Hildy had plenty of experience presenting cases to juries, but it's different when what you're selling is yourself. Oh well, I thought, that's not my problem. After all, I've seen very little evidence that the meek will inherit the earth.

Uncharacteristically, and for this occasion only, I'm sure, Jeff was seated at a front table. In fact, he was the only person seated at the table when I whispered to him, still holding my bowl and plate, "She looks kind of nervous, don't you think?"

Jeff is not a good whisperer, probably because he doesn't hear well himself. He made a show of speaking into his hand, but between his looking directly at Hildy as he spoke and his volume, I'm sure Hildy heard Jeff say, "Yeah, I was just thinking she looks like fucking Peter Cottontail in MacGregor's garden. Go make a fucking pie out of her, big boy!"

In a diversionary effort, I smiled faintly and directed my gaze toward someone eating salad at another table, but I have no doubt Hildy took in the whole scene and was offended. Demonstrating to Jeff how one whispers, I quietly said to him, still looking away from Hildy, "Nice going, asshole. Now you've pissed her off before we've even started."

"What did I do?" said Jeff.

"Forget it."

I walked up to the dais and set down my food. I took two steps toward where Hildy sat on the other side of the microphone and stuck out my hand.

"Hildegarde," I said, "I know we've met before, but I just wanted to say hello. I'm sorry we have to meet again under these circumstances."

Hildy dabbed her mouth with her napkin, stood up, and gave me one of those bony, too-firm handshakes that professional women think they're supposed to give when they shake hands with a man, so he'll note how strong she is. She even held onto my hand for minute and leaned into me to speak toward my right ear.

"Oh, Norman," Hildy said, "I know what you mean. I wish there were a different way to select judges. I think you'd make an excellent judge, and I just hate it that only one of us will be able to serve. You'd think we could have come up with a better way. I mean, it would be a lot easier to talk to strangers than a roomful of lawyers we both know, don't you think? But I guess if we can do this, we can talk to anybody, right?"

Hildy was speaking urgently and quickly. She seemed to be talking herself into a panic, and I actually patted her hand, which was still grasping mine, with my free hand.

"Yeah," I said, trying to sound soothing and confident, "I agree. I wish there were another way. But, hey, whatever happens, we'll just be professional about it, and people will vote how they vote. It's not like the voters even know who the damn judicial candidates are, anyway. Whatever happens will have everything to do with the county's population demographics and nothing to do with us."

I noticed that Hildy winced when I had said "damn," and she didn't nod her head in agreement with my assessment of the race. Oh well.

"Well, anyway," Hildy said, finally releasing my hand, "good luck. Do you want the rest of my salad? I'm too nervous to eat."

I assured Hildy I had plenty to eat, but thanked her and sat down, thinking of the contrast this audience, and future political audiences, would see between the nervous, timid Hildegarde Pierce, and the confident but charming Norman Spiczek. I could even afford to be self-deprecating so it wouldn't look like I was bullying the poor woman.

Linda Winegarten, this year's chair of the section, took her place behind the microphone and tried to quiet the audience. If you've ever tried to get a roomful of lawyers to stop talking, you will understand the difficulty of her task. If you haven't, imagine being in a rainforest with about 5,000 birds and other animals screeching out their varied calls and saying, "Okay, everybody, we're about to start, so please take your seats. Hello, everybody? We're ready to get started. May I have your attention please?"

There was no discernable decrease in the din, but Linda had the good sense to declare victory and move forward, just as if she had been effective. She made a few general announcements along the lines of court policies that had become effective only last month that were being altered by some of the courts but not all of them, and the court clerks had asked for an announcement, once again, that they would really appreciate it if lawyers would use a two-hole punch in their documents so they could be more easily filed in the courts' jackets. Once again, as in all previous meetings with this same announcement, the lawyers ignored the request.

Then Linda said we would begin the candidates' forum and explained the rules. (Lawyers, of course, must have rules, and they'd probably been hashed out extensively over many objections and amendments at the last meeting of the Board of Directors of the Family Law Section). Each candidate would have three minutes (with an allowed runover of one minute) to speak about him or herself. The candidates were not to address each other as this forum was not intended to be a debate. Two questions for each candidate would be allowed from the floor. In other words, this was to be quite the sanitized affair, and I couldn't help noticing Stanley Canon rolling his eyes at a table near the back of the room and then glance at the door, apparently planning his escape.

"Okay everyone," Linda said, "I think most everyone everyone here knows our two candidates for the 404th Court. We'll start with Hildegarde Pierce."

Linda motioned Hildy toward the microphone, and after one more dab with the napkin, Hildy stood up and approached the microphone behind the wooden lectern. Man, I felt nervous *for* her.

Hildy's voice, though, didn't sound at all shaky when she began speaking, and the few people who had continued their conversations during Linda's attempts to gain order now quieted down and turned toward Hildy at the front of the room.

"Ladies and gentlemen, my name is Hildegarde Pierce, and before I tell you what the 404th Family District Court needs, let me tell you what it doesn't need. It doesn't need what my opponent has to offer."

Hildy actually sneered as she spoke that last sentence. You really don't see too many good sneers in a post-vaudeville world, but she pulled it off nicely. Now everyone, including me, was staring at Hildy with rapt attention, and some mouths in the audience were beginning to drop open, including, I noted with irritation, the corpulent one of Jeff, still sitting alone right in front of the dais. People were spellbound by this departure from the routine, and Hildy was just warming up.

"This court doesn't need," Hildy continued, "a soulless, money-chasing shark who thinks this profession's highest aspiration is the Almighty Dollar. Frankly, I think University Park's residents are already sufficiently represented, and the real working people of this county need a judge who will make sure fairness and justice do not depend on how much you can pay for a lawyer.

Going back to my direct ancestor, President Franklin Pierce, my family has given of itself to make this a better country for everyone. I want to continue that tradition, in my own humble way, by serving Dallas County as the next judge of the 404th Court. I intend to proudly continue the moral values expounded for the last 20 years by Judge Curtis, and I will proudly tell you right now that my priorities have always been, and always will be, my God, my country, and the law. That may sound old-fashioned to some of you, but that's just the way I was raised, and I will never apologize for my moral compass.

My values have served me well in my career as a prosecutor for this county, and I am proud that I have risen to the top position in the DA's office in charge of all prosecutors in the Child Protective Services cases. Sure, I haven't made the money that my colleagues in private practice have made over the years (Hildy glanced my way) but I never felt like I have sacrificed anything. In fact, my riches lie elsewhere (and yes, she actually glanced up toward the ceiling). I promise I will serve you well as a judge. Thank you, and I'd be glad to turn over the remainder of my time to Mr. Spiczek."

The lawyers who were not stunned motionless applauded Hildy with gusto as she primly resumed her seat. Perhaps unconsciously, she dabbed at her mouth again with her napkin, possibly to soak up some stray venom that had spewed from her lips.

Linda Winegarten looked a bit flustered as she approached the microphone, and I shared her feeling. I felt the...what is it, bile, gall...rise in my chest and throat as I belatedly absorbed the sneak attack from Hildegard Pierce.

"And now, everyone, Norm." Linda wrinkled her brow, knowing she'd made some sort of mistake, and then leaned into the microphone again. "I mean, Norman Spiczek, everyone."

The room was deadly quiet now, as I bent the neck of the microphone stand higher, causing it to emit a screeching sound over the speakers. I glanced at Jeff, who seemed to have recovered from Hildy's lightening-quick onslaught. He discreetly punched his right hand into his left in a "give her hell" gesture.

I paused a beat, let the audience become aware of the silence, and then made a show of crumpling the piece of paper I had before me and tossing it over my shoulder to the floor.

"I've decided to forego the use of my notes and speak to you directly from my money-grubbing, shrunken black heart. (A couple of nervous, twitchy laughs were released around the room). What a load of crap you just heard. (Some raised eyebrows, a few smiles, and one "Damn right" muttered loudly by Jeff). Gee, I'm sorry to say that I don't come from a long line of political hacks leading all the way back to an obscure president whom nobody remembers. No, my ancestors were busy escaping the totalitarian horrors of Europe so they could build a better life in the land of opportunity, working their way from the bottom up in this society, and that's just what they did." (Well, actually, I think my mother's side of the family owned a slave or two in North Carolina, but I'd never looked into it too carefully. But if I remember correctly, my father's ancestors were from Poland, or Czechoslovakia, or some such place with a lot of consonants. Odds are they were oppressed).

"I suppose Ms. Pierce would like me to apologize for my success in private practice as a lawyer, but in fact I'm quite proud of it. I started a business where there was none, made a name and a career for myself among my competitors, generated taxable revenue (I glanced at Hildy with what I hoped looked like contempt, but I wouldn't try a sneer until I could practice in front of a mirror) and employment that hadn't existed until

I created it. Along with my spouse (another glance at Hildy), I have supported a household and raised a daughter without gulping from the public trough, and, yes, I've done well. Yes, it's true that the courthouse sits at the corner of Market and Commerce streets, but I have always known that practicing law is about more than making money.

Still, I'm proud to say that I've done well enough that now I believe it's time for me to give back to my community in a tangible way. Ms. Pierce is right about one thing. Becoming your next judge, which I plan to do, will mean a pay cut for me, and the first time in my life that I've been paid by you, the taxpayers, to do my job. So unlike Ms. Pierce, I am making a sacrifice, but it's one I freely make, and I will make damn sure the county gets its money's worth from a public servant who knows what it means to work hard for a living. If you'd like to ask any questions that actually have to do with the duties of a judge, I'd be happy to change the subject to that. Thank you."

Yes! I heard plenty of applause as I sat down, and when Jeff stood up and clapped his hands vigorously over his head as if he were at a rock concert, a couple of other people stood up as well. I knew them both, and they were good friends. Many people were staring at the microphone as if someone were still there talking, and a few others sat with their arms crossed. How could I gauge the reaction to what had just played out?

Linda looked scared as she approached the microphone again and pulled the neck back down to her mouth level.

"Um," she said, "that was, uh, very spirited. Does anyone have any questions for our, uh, candidates?"

Oh Lord, Renee Lithwigger stood up, all 250 antagonistic pounds of her, and started talking. Renee didn't need a microphone to be heard.

"Yeah," Renee began, missing only the rolling caption beneath her image to look and sound exactly like an audience member from Jerry Springer. "I want to ask the prosecutor what she's got against lawyers in private practice trying to make a living? Does that mean you'll never grant attorney's fees, no matter how egregious the conduct of the other lawyer?"

There was a smattering of applause as Renee remained standing, hand on her jutting hip, demanding an answer.

Okay, then, I thought, this is going well. Hildy approached the microphone.

"If attorney's fees are warranted, they will absolutely be ordered. I will not tolerate abusive behavior, or (and here she looked at me again) incivility in my courtroom, and if it happens, it will be punished appropriately. *I* will run my courtroom, not a group of good old boys who have come to think they own the place."

Jesus, I think she means me! Good old boy? I don't even own a pair of cowboy boots. I drive a Volvo.

The cheers for Hildy's answer were solid and enthusiastic. And then I saw Judge Curtis for the first time, who'd been sitting off to the side of the room. He stood up, walked a few paces toward the center, and politely raised his hand to get Linda's attention. He was stooped over, and he looked older and frailer than I'd ever seen him. He was striking this vulnerable pose for dramatic purposes, the bastard.

Linda spotted him. "Oh, yes, Judge Curtis, did you want to ask a question?"

Curtis actually performed a half-bow toward Linda. It looked creepy, like Vincent Price.

"Yes, if I may, Madame Chairwoman. I hope I'm not out of order here to say that I was very impressed by Ms. Pierce's comments, and I would be proud to have her follow me on the bench of the 404th. I just hope she won't be too disturbed to have to look at a photograph of homely old me on the wall of the courtroom everyday."

The whole room laughed approvingly at the self-deprecating, charming old man. *I* was supposed to be the charming, self-deprecating one, goddamn it.

"And, of course," Curtis finished, "I extend my best wishes to Mr. Spick-zek as well."

That bastard had pronounced my name correctly for years, and now he gets it wrong? Damn him.

I fairly leaped from my seat toward the microphone and was reaching to jerk up its neck when Linda, with uncharacteristic aggressiveness, stepped in front of me.

"I'm sorry, Norman, but our time is up for today. Thank you all for coming, and we'll see you next month."

The room erupted into a cacophony of conversation as seemingly everyone began talking to each other at once, and I was left standing at the lectern, looking, or at least feeling, foolish.

"Fine," I snarled in Linda's direction, and walked quickly down the steps of the raised dais. Jeff was there to greet me.

"What the hell was that?" is how I greeted Jeff. "Where does that bitch get off acting all holier-than-thou? And that thing with Curtis. That had to be set up. What a bunch of shit."

Jeff put his hand on my shoulder. "Whoa, Elvis, let's talk about this later. Just smile and shake some hands for now. And try to be nicer. Remember, you're the Democrat here."

CHAPTER FIFTEEN

I was eating dinner with Loren and Elizabeth at Serendipity, a "relaxed casual dining experience," if one were to believe the advertising. After my experience with Hildy and the family law bar at lunch, I needed a little relaxed dining, but what I really needed was the Jack on the rocks sitting in front of me.

After I had related to Loren the unexpectedness, and viciousness, of Hildy's attack on me, Elizabeth, who had been coloring in one of the coloring books Loren always kept in her purse for these occasions, paused in her work to look up at me.

"You know, Dad," said my five-year-old daughter. "We're meat, but we look like bread."

With drink in hand, I squinted at my daughter. No matter how many times Elizabeth came up with these bizarre observations, they still took me by surprise. Something odd had happened when Loren and I had conceived this little human, but it was a marvelous kind of odd.

"What kind of bread?" was all I could think to ask.

"Different kinds," Elizabeth said, and looked back down at her coloring book. "Sometimes that wheat kind, and sometimes the Wonder Bread kind. Some people have nuts and stuff in them. Some have crusts, some don't."

"And some are sour dough, evidently," Loren added. "Like Ms. Pierce."

"She's a bit nutty, too," I added, sipping from my drink.

Loren expressed surprise that a candidates' forum in front of a group of lawyers would get so heated.

"It sounds more like a presidential debate than a judicial race," Loren said.

"Exactly. That's what I thought. I've never seen anything like it, and what makes it even weirder is how nice she was just before she started in on me. I mean, the whole thing was just so premeditated. And I know Curtis' comments weren't just off the cuff. He and Hildy must have concocted that whole thing. I don't think I've even seen Curtis at one of those meetings in years."

"So what does Jeff recommend?" asked Loren.

"He can't seem to make up his mind. First he told me to just be myself, then he told me to be nice. So which is it, I asked him."

Between Loren's smile and the warm spread of alcohol through my body, I was beginning to relax and put the day's activity in perspective. It's a shame that I'd come to rely on a glass or two of liquor to calm me down most evenings, but what the hell, I didn't get rip-snorting drunk and I didn't use heavier drugs, so it could be worse. If we can just manage our vices effectively and avoid hurting other people with them, we're doing okay. My personal philosophy in this area was sort of a cross between Buddhism and surrender. Maybe it was an ethical rationalization, or maybe I just liked my whiskey.

"So what's next?" Loren asked.

"Jeff wants me to go to this meeting of Democratic precinct chairs next week. He's right, I'm sure. I need to show my face at these things, get to be known by the party loyalists. Of course, I think a lot of that is overrated. After all, it isn't the Democrats I need to convince to vote for a Democrat, it's the Independents and hopefully a few Republicans. And really, looking on the bright side, if Hildy's going to be such a...(I glanced at my daughter, coloring away)...so unpleasant about all this, it kind of frees me up to say what I really think about things. If she were exceedingly polite and nice about everything, I'd probably have to be the same way."

Loren finished chewing and pointed her fork at me for emphasis as she spoke.

"That's true, but I think Jeff's right. You have to be careful. It may be a double standard, but the world's full of double standards, and this is one of the few that operate in favor of women and against men. Even if she attacks you, you have to respond forcefully, but you can't appear to be a bully. If you remain polite and logical while she gets more personal, then you'll get the benefit of the stereotype that women are hysterical and men remain calm under pressure."

"That's a stereotype? Just kidding," I said. "Don't get hysterical. But you're right. It's all about perception. Besides, the general public couldn't care less about judicial races. Nobody cares who the judges are until they have to come before one, and then it's too late. So I'll just let Hildy play her little game of trying to paint me as some out-of-touch capitalist pig, and I'll talk about being a judge. Now that I know what to expect from her, I think I can handle it."

But in life, as in golf, one never really knows what's coming next.

Thus it was that I was taken aback by the meeting the next week of the Democratic precinct chairs. I expected maybe a dozen people to show up at the union hall where Jeff told me to be. Instead, there must have been around 70 to 80 people sitting in folding metal chairs in a big room that had boxes shoved to one side and which obviously served as a storage room of some sort when it didn't have metal chairs and card tables set up for a meeting. One table had a sad looking bowl of pretzel sticks dumped in it, and someone had bought a package of cupcakes with bright-colored icing from a grocery store. There were a few flattened-out homemade peanut butter and jelly sandwiches, divided between two plates. In front of each plate of the PB&Js was a hand-lettered piece of cardstock, one of which said, "Crusts" and the other said "No-Crusts." A third hand-lettered card said, "Attention: contains wheat and peanuts." Well, no shit, I thought.

And if anyone thought I was being elitist for not scooping out some pretzel sticks from the community bowl where I'd just seen a man named Charlie (or at least that's what the sewn-in name tag on his blue shirt said) dip his grease-marked fingers, then let them think it. I poured what appeared to be cherry Kool-Aid from a plastic pitcher into a paper cup, took one sip, and tried to find a place to get rid of the cup without being noticed. At least I'd had the foresight to remove my tie before I came in, thinking it would give me a "man of the people" look.

As I found a seat near the middle of the room and sat down, I saw Jeff approaching me with a plate.

"Hey," Jeff said, "there you are. Did you see they have pretzel sticks? I love those things. Hold this while I sit down." Jeff handed me his plate and made a grunting sound as he lowered himself onto the metal chair next to me.

Jeff looked around appraisingly, as he took the plate of pretzel sticks and two PB&Js back from me.

"This is a good venue," he said. "Oh, here, I've got something for you. You need to wear this."

Jeff handed me a square of plastic with a safety pin in the back and writing on the front that said, "Norman Spiczek, Candidate, 404th Family Cort."

I held the name tag in my hand like he'd handed me petrified dog shit from his yard.

" 'Court' is misspelled. I can't wear this," I said.

"Don't worry. We got a discount." Jeff shoved some pretzel sticks in his mouth but that didn't keep him from talking around them. "I bought a dozen of them, so we can pass them out. I'm putting one on now."

Jeff pulled one of the pins out of his pocket and fastened it to his shirt at a lopsided angle.

I sighed and carefully affixed my own to my shirt, thinking about the damage I was doing to the expensive Italian shirt that Loren had purchased for me at Neimans, as well as the damage to my dignity.

A few people were still milling around but most had taken their seats. I saw a man approach the front of the room and stand behind the card table that had been set up there. When he spoke, I knew I recognized the voice, but I couldn't immediately place it.

"Okay, everyone, let's take our places. One must start a meeting in a timely fashion if one expects to complete it in a timely fashion."

Stokely. Jeff leaned over to me, and whisper-shouted in my ear, "That's Walter Stokely. He's the..."

"I know," I whispered back.

Walter Stokely was a toadlike man, shortish (maybe 5'5", tops), roundish, crammed into a brown suit that looked like it came from Sears a few years ago, when he was less round. He wore frameless glasses with thick lenses that did nothing to diminish his toadlike aspect. Yet he held himself with such affected dignity that it became pomposity in his body language, standing up straight, head and shoulders back, doing his best to look down on everyone, which he was able to do only because everyone else was sitting while he stood. I think I hated him.

"I believe each of us here knows each of the others," began Stokely, in his whiny, high-pitched voice that began and ended in his nose, "and so I shall hereby call this meeting of the Dallas County Democratic Party to order, based upon the authority vested in me by virtue of my current position as Chairperson of the Party." He really liked saying that, you could tell.

"We do have Party business to conduct," Stokely continued, "but if I may be so bold (and here he adjusted his glasses), I would like to seek permission to allow a special guest to address us first. One may presume that this special guest is very busy and may not have the time to stay for the entire meeting. As much as I would like to expedite matters by moving for this exception myself (Stokely chuckled as if he'd said something witty), one knows that the Chairperson is not allowed by our bylaws to introduce motions, except in special circumstances described therein. (He chuckled again. Stokely really cracked himself up. The fact that there were a few other chuckles around the room at this non-humor began to worry me). So might I ask that one of my comrades here make said motion?"

It occurred to me that Democrats should never use the word "comrades." Talk about unnecessary connotations.

A woman of about 27 who could have passed for 57 for her apparent lifelong lack of make-up and the burlap sack she used as a dress stood up. If I had been closer to her, I could probably have seen the bugs jumping out of her hair, but I was glad that I was not.

"I so move that we allow the special guest mentioned by Chairperson Stokely to speak out of order," said the Woman of the Hills.

Charlie the Mechanic, with his beefy forearms crossed over his gut, stood up and barked out, "I second the motion." I had no idea Roberts Rules of Order were so popular.

"Excellent," Grandmaster Stokely said, actually rubbing together his dry little hands. "The motion is carried. Let me introduce to our humble group a man who has graced us with his presence tonight and let him explain what brings him here. I'm sure he will be glad to entertain questions from any of you who may have them. Mr. Norman Spiczek, would you please do us the honor?" For the first time during the meeting, Stokely looked directly at me, revealing that he'd known I was present all along.

What a little shit.

As eyes turned toward me from around the room, I stood up walked to the front. Stokely stuck out his stubby arm and shook my hand, saying loudly enough for the people in the first few rows to hear that he was glad to finally meet me. More quietly, he said to me, "Dazzle us." I returned his handshake and simply said "Thanks."

Addressing the audience, I began.

"Well, I wasn't expecting to speak at this evening's meeting, but I'm glad for the opportunity. Yes, as your, our, Chairman said, I'm running for the judge of the 404th Family District Court. For those who may not know, it's a countywide court with specific jurisdiction over family law matters like divorces, child custody and child support, visitation issues, uh, cases involving child welfare…"

I had just started, and I could see I was losing the audience. Jeff was making some sort of signal to me with his hands, like a "pump it up" sort of gesture. And then he stuffed some more pretzel sticks in his mouth.

I stopped speaking for a moment and just looked out at the audience.

"Okay, you probably don't care what the 404th Court does. If you do, you can ask me about it later. Let's talk about something more important, like why Democrats keep losing elections to Republicans. Some people (I quickly glanced at Walter Stokely) work really hard in the party, I know, and they may resent someone like me running for an office when I haven't been seen doing much of the dirty work. (I saw some nodding heads).

Well, that's understandable, but some of us are better and more motivated to do that kind of stuff than others. Frankly, although I've been a loyal Democratic voter since I was 18, I'd never really considered running for any office myself until just recently. Those of you who can get over your resentment will do so; those of you who can't, won't. So be it. Let's move on.

I've already discovered that my Republican opponent for this bench intends to play the God card, the class card, make shows of patriotism, and anything else she can pull from the pre-stocked bag of Republican garbage that her party has been using for years. And you know why she will? Because it works. The Republicans don't have better ideas than we do, they just sell their same old divisive trash better than we can sell hope. (Now I saw some stirring in the crowd).

In fact, you know what the real difference is between most Republicans and most Democrats? Democrats try to educate the voters. Republicans try to take advantage of voters' pre-existing ignorance. So which approach do you think works better? Democrats are always telling people that they don't know enough and need to learn. Republicans keep telling people they know all they need to know and that the Democrats are just trying to confuse them. People would rather hear that they're plenty smart than that they aren't smart enough.

But don't think the Democrats have been blameless in their own demise. I'm sick and tired of this party trying to play Republican Lite, going around just mimicking what the Republicans say and trying to be convincing. If they say they love their country, we say 'Well, we do, too.' (And here I imitated a bit of a sniveling tone of voice, not unlike that of Walter Stokely). "They say, 'we have moral values,' and like trained seals we bark back, "Well, so do we."

Look, the fact is, a lot of voters out there are stupid, lazy and selfish. (Angry murmurs, people looking at each other. Jeff made a throat-slitting gesture now). Oh, come on, you know it's true. But, hey, the people who *don't* vote, which is the majority, can be even stupider and lazier. We've got to find a way to reach *them*. These are the people who make their decisions on whom to vote for, or to vote at all, based on appearance, name value, and who seems like they might be fun to have a beer with. They don't read newspapers, and they barely watch the drivel that passes for local TV news. So it would be great if I could impress the committed party types like the people in this room, but even if I did, I would be just another in a long line of noble losers. So, sure, I'd like to have the support of the local Democratic Party, but there aren't enough of you to make or break my campaign, so please don't take it personally if I concentrate my efforts elsewhere.

My campaign manager is an amateur at this political stuff, also. He's sitting right there, Jeff Frankel. (People turned to look where I pointed, catching Jeff in the middle of a more-urgent throat-slashing gesture, and with a mouthful of pretzel sticks. Forgetting to lower his hand, he smiled weakly at the audience). I can see that Jeff is getting concerned about my impromptu speech, so I'll cut it short now. Thank you for your attention."

About 20 of the 80 or so people in the room fairly leapt from their seats and applauded loudly. The rest remained seated. I heard at least two or three actual boos, like we were at a Rangers game. At least no one had any beer to throw at me.

Some individuals seemed to want to approach and talk to me. But as they stood up to do so, Walter Stokely surprised me by speaking louder and more strongly than I would have thought him capable.

"People, people. Please come to order. After that enlightening speech by one of our down-ballot candidates, we have some real business to conduct. Take your seats now, please."

And they did. The individuals who had stood up and started coming my way turned back around and resumed sitting on their folding metal chairs as if their second grade teacher had scolded them. I looked at Jeff and said, "Let's go," nodding toward the door.

As Jeff and I walked quickly to the door in the back of the room, Jeff said, "Do you think they'd mind if I took some pretzel sticks to go?"

CHAPTER SIXTEEN

I was on the phone with Jeff, talking from my office downtown.

"You have a stange way of building coalitions, *amigo*," Jeff said. "But I have to admit, I did enjoy it, retrospectively more than at the moment."

"Yeah, well, Stokely kind of pissed me off. Still, though, I don't regret it. If I'd had more time to prepare, I may not have said things the way I did, but I really mean what I said. Well, I mean, to the extent I remember what all I said."

"Um, well," Jeff said, "you basically told the Democratic Party of Dallas County to go to hell. The weird part is that some of them applauded you for saying it."

"Well, that kind of figures," I said.

"But here's what I'm really calling about," Jeff went on. "I got a call from the paper, a reporter whose divorce I handled a few years ago, and we've kind of kept in touch every now and then. He heard about the Party meeting, and he'd like to hear you the next time you talk. So it looks like the beginning of some buzz, and that means free advertising. Given how warmly you deal with not only your opponent but your so-called supporters, too, I don't know how much publicity I want you to have, but what the hell, at least we'll get your name out there. Of course, it necessarily means Hildy's name will be put out there, too."

"What *is* the next time I talk, anyway?"

"A week from this Sunday, you and Hildy have been invited to speak together at the Methodist church out north on Hillcrest. I've already accepted for you," Jeff said. "It's in the afternoon."

"When do the Cowboys play that day?" I asked, reasonably I thought. "I'm closer to the Cowboys than to the Methodists."

"I don't know, but you can record it. This is a good opportunity."

"It's not the same when you record it," I said. "First, you have to worry that someone will come running in with an update on the game before you can put your hands over your ears, and even if you manage to avoid that, and you watch the recording later, you know in the back of your mind that what you're watching has already happened. I really hate that. It's like having sex with your wife and being distracted by thinking about all the people she's had sex with before you, you know what I mean?"

"No," Jeff said, "I have no idea what you mean. So, anyway, put that on your calendar. It's for that Sunday at 1:30."

"Is this a religious thing?" I asked. "It's at the church."

"No, I don't think it's religious, Norm. Methodists vote as well as pray, you know. And it's open to anyone who wants to come. I don't think they'll have guards checking your Methodist ID card at the door. Besides, these are the North Dallas voters you said you need to reach."

I sighed and told Jeff I'd be there. Missing the Cowboys game really pissed me off, even though they'd probably lose anyway.

My intercom buzzed, and it was Vivian.

"Norm, may I come in and talk to you a minute about Gloria Stapleton?"

I told Vivian to come on back, and she took her accustomed seat on the couch. Isn't it odd how territorial we are? Even in college, when there was no assigned seating, once I sat in a chair on the first day of class, I always returned to that same chair for the rest of the semester. "Floaters," people who intentionally sat in different parts of the classroom "just to change things up," got on my last nerve. I guess that's just one more way to differentiate people in this world: you have your "floaters," and you have your "anchors." Vivian and I were both anchors.

Gloria Stapleton was an anchor plunging to the bottom.

Vivian recounted to me her recent telephone conversation with the client.

"I called her yesterday afternoon to tell her that I'd received some discovery requests from her husband's attorney, and Gloria burst into tears like I'd told her one of her kids had died," Vivian said. "I mean, hell, Norm, they were just routine discovery requests, you know, nothing that should cause a nervous breakdown. I don't know what to do with her. She kept asking me, 'Can't we just get this over? Why must we drag it out?' I didn't have the heart to tell her that, as divorce cases go, it's flying along quite nicely."

I steepled my hands in front of my chin and trapped a sigh there.

"All right, here's what we're gonna do," I said. "We're going to use Gloria's fragile mental state to her advantage. If she ever comes out of her emotional coma, she may thank us one day. Let's get Gloria's husband's attorney on the phone. Who is it?"

"Samantha Drinkwater," Vivian replied.

"Okay, she's pretty reasonable, I think we can work with her. What I want to do is convince Samantha that it's in the husband's best interests to come up with a very generous offer to Gloria right now before our client completely collapses, because at that point this case will be delayed indefinitely, and the heartless philanderer may have to take care of his inconvenient old wife for a lot longer than he'd care to. It seems to me that hubby's in a big hurry to move on to his new girl, don't you think?"

Vivian agreed. According to what Gloria had told Vivian, Stephen was so wrapped up in his girlfriend that he didn't even call the kids, including Bethany who had just started college and was quite distraught over the divorce. Their other kid, Mark, refused to speak to his father because he was so angry with him.

"Okay, good," I said, "we can use his kids' well-being against him, too."

Vivian wrinkled her face like she'd smelled something unpleasant.

"Well," I backtracked, "I don't mean *"good"* good, just good in that it will help me get a better deal for our client." Vivian hadn't been practicing family law long enough to use the shorthand speech that veteran family law attorneys employ, like "*Yes*, I got a wife of 35 years who's husband left the videotape of himself having sex with the babysitter in the fucking VCR! Can you believe my good luck? Balls to the wall on this one, baby!" Every profession has a version of this, doesn't it?

"Anyway," I continued, "let's get Samantha on the phone."

Vivian called Samantha's office, and after the requisite time on hold necessary to show us that Samantha Drinkwater was a busy attorney who couldn't just drop everything to talk to anyone who called, Samantha came on the line.

"Hi, Samantha, this is Vivian at Norman Spizcek's office (I can't help it, I still liked the sound of that, it was so grown-up), and I have Norm here on speakerphone as well. We're calling about the Stapleton case."

"Hi, Vivian, hi, Norm," Samantha cooed over the line.

I'm not sure what I'd rather deal with, attorneys who are all nasty all the time, or the sickly sweet, two-faced type like Samantha who would smile and make kissy talk while she lied about you and your client to you, the judge, the court reporter, and homeless people on the courthouse elevators who'd just come in to take a bath in the sink. At least with the first group, you knew where you stood. The problem with Samantha's type is that they'd never met a client who wasn't the most honest, unfairly-treated, and reasonable person in the world, and Samantha couldn't understand when everyone else didn't see things her client's way, too.

"Hey, Samantha," I said. "Listen, I want to talk to you about where we're going with this case." It was best, when dealing with Samantha Drinkwater, to get right down to business before she asked about kids, pets, the weather, whatever could lengthen a telephone conversation and allow her to bill more hours. "My concern is..."

"How's that precious little girl of yours?" Samantha interrupted.

Vivian rolled her eyes, but damn it, Samantha didn't fight fair. It felt like a betrayal of Elizabeth to ignore Samantha's compliment.

"Um, well, she's precious, I guess." Vivian made the universal rolling hand gensture that means, "move along now."

"But anyway," I continued, narrowing my eyes in Vivian's direction, "because we're friends, Samantha, I wanted to warn you about a problem I see develping in the Stapleton case." Ha, two could play this game.

"That's so sweet, Norm. I don't know how you even find time to practice law while you're running for judge. You must be so busy."

"Oh, I find the time when I need to," I said. "Has your client mentioned to you anything about my client's emotional state?"

Samantha took the bait. "As a matter of fact, he has. Between you and me, Norm, and Vivian, too, of course, I think it's one of the reasons he left her. She's really unstable. I don't know how the poor man put up with her as long as he did. I mean, she's kind of a basket case, know what I mean? Stephen was only thinking about their kids when he stayed with Gloria as long as he did."

Good, I had her. "Well," I said, winking at Vivian as I did so, "he might have had a thought or two about his new girlfriend, as well, but who am I to quibble? The thing is, Stephen is exactly right. Gloria is a mess, quite frankly, and I'm just glad for my client that custody isn't an issue. What *is* an issue is alimony, and I thought it was only fair to tell you, in case Stephen hadn't, just what bad shape Gloria is in. Like your client told you, Gloria is unstable, probably far worse than when Stephen left her for his girlfriend, know what I mean?"

Samantha was catching on. "Now, Norman, I don't think…"

I plowed ahead. "What I would like to avoid, Samantha, is the ugliness of taking the girlfriend's deposition and Stephen's deposition, and just the whole sordidness of their affair. I mean, it's really put Gloria over the edge, and to get her alimony beyond the statutory maximum of 20 percent of gross for three years, I'd have to show how callous Stephen was and the devastating effect he's had on Gloria. I mean, really, Samantha, this is a woman who's been at home for the last 18 years, and

I sure don't see her being able to secure a decent job any time soon. Not with her lack of business experience combined with her emotional fragility. Know what I mean?"

It was hard to finish my sentence without breaking up, as Vivian had her hand over her mouth and was making grunting noises to choke back her own laughter. This proved once again that the simple things in life that made you laugh when you were 10 could still do so after you pass 40.

The suppressed antics of Vivian and me gave Samantha a chance to jump in.

"Norman, I don't think...I mean...well, look, your client has got to realize that things are about to change for her. I mean, the gravy train is over. She's got to..."

I interrupted again, and said, helpfully I thought, "Oh, Samantha, for Stephen's sake, please don't use the 'gravy train' expression in court. You know how sensitive judges can be these days. And besides, like you said, Gloria's been going downhill for years, not just since her husband abandoned her, although that sure didn't help. If there are any train analogies here, it's that Stephen rode the Gloria train right into the ground, and now he just wants to scoot her off onto a siding and let her rust out while he gets himself a shiny, new locomotive."

"That's a good train analogy," said Vivian, standing beside me.

"Thanks, Vivian," I said into the speakerphone. It felt like Vivian and I were lobbing rehearsed lines at each other in an infomercial. Maybe it was time to talk to Samantha again.

"Anyway, Samantha, we go back a long way, and I didn't want to spring all this on you without telling you first. I think cooperation is the best way to operate, don't you? Maybe you should discuss it with Stephen and get back to me, but you'll have to do it by tomorrow because, frankly, I feel like we're holding Gloria together right now with Scotch tape and paper clips. For Stephen's sake, it would be a lot cleaner if we got this divorce wrapped up before Gloria has to be institutionalized."

Vivian made a hand gesture that could have meant that I'd gone "over the top" or that I was "falling flat," but she was silently laughing as she made it.

It was Samantha who let out a mirthless chuckle sound and said, "Well, Norm, that's a lot to absorb. Let me talk to Stephen. He can be hard to reach sometimes, so it may be a few days."

"Oh, man, I wish we had a few days, Samantha, but I can't guarantee to you that I can wait that long. You'd better ask Stephen how he thinks Gloria's doing. I think he'll tell you that *his* future looks a lot brighter than Gloria's."

As we said our goodbyes, and Vivian and I retold the story of the just-completed conversation in a way that suggested to me it would quickly become part of office lore, I thought, "That's how I like my confrontations. Sideways, not head-on, and wrapped in a smile and a wink."

CHAPTER SEVENTEEN

Head-on confrontations, though, are what politics is all about, and the candidates' forum at the Methodist church was bearing down on me. It was the Tuesday morning before the Sunday afternoon of the forum when Jeff called me on my cell phone as I was driving to the courthouse for a divorce "prove-up."

A "prove-up" is a routine appearance before the court to finalize a case that had already been agreed to and signed off on by all parties and their attorneys. All that was left was to stand in front of a judge with your client and ask him or her a few questions under oath, like "Is that really your signature?" and my favorite, which established "no-fault" grounds: "Isn't it true that the marriage has become insupportable because of discord or conflict of personalities that destroys the legitimate ends of the marital relationship and prevents any reasonable expectation of reconciliation?"

Any family lawyer with more than two years experience could rattle off that compound, leading question with such little attention to it that the lawyer could think about where she was going for lunch that day or the stain on his tie even as the polysyllabic words spilled forth. Usually I had Vivian cover prove-ups for me at this stage of my practice, but she had a hearing of her own this morning, and doing the occasional prove-up kept me humble, I thought, although to think you are humble is to not be humble, by definition.

Still, every once in awhile I actually gave some thought to the big prove-up question, and I thought, "What the hell *are* the legitimate ends of the marital relationship, anyway?" It was a decent bit of prose for statutory language cranked out by our legislators in Austin, and I wondered if an English major who was serving as an aide to a state rep had come up with it. I especially liked that last bit: "reasonable expectation of reconciliation." The phrase has a Latin heft to it.

"What are you doing a prove-up for?" asked Jeff. "I thought you had people for that."

"My 'people' is doing something else this morning. Besides, I don't mind doing the occasional prove-up; it keeps me humble," I said.

"Bullshit." It's a sign of a good friendship that your buddy can call you out immediately on a falsity and neither of you takes it personally. I'll never know for sure, but I suspect the dialogue between two women, no matter how friendly, would not have gone the same way.

After making his cogent analysis of my claim to humility, Jeff continued. "Hey, we've got that reporter from the 'Magnifier' showing up at the forum Sunday. Isn't that cool?"

"The Magnifier," aptly named, was a weekly, free "newspaper" that showed up around town every Tuesday and was supported by personal ads along the lines of "Bi/Hetero M, seeking Straight Ms, or Trans, any race, 18 to 65, for mutually-fulfilling adventures in water and space. No tattoos." "The Magnifier" tended to inflate ordinary stories each week with headlines like last week's: "Meet the Dallas Cop Who Hates Dallas Cops." A debate between a couple of judicial candidates didn't sound like their kind of story, and I said so to Jeff.

"Well," Jeff said, "Remember, I handled this reporter's divorce awhile back, and he owes me. And it's possible that

I mentioned the fireworks from the last time you and Hildy locked horns and told him he could expect more of the same."

"God, you're such a pimp," I said, just before pulling into the courthouse's underground parking garage and losing cell phone contact.

"Yeah, but if I'm the pimp, what would that make you?" Jeff said.

The prove-up itself was as uneventful as expected, it being the culmination of a divorce case in which the husband (our client) and his wife had made an amicable split of their modest estate and agreed to allow the wife to be the primary conservator of their three children, with visitation rights for the husband. It had been easy to settle because it wasn't like our client, Stan, really wanted the kids full-time anyway, and the two of them made about equal salaries. Stan would pay his wife child support according to the state's guidelines, based on his income. This was the kind of marriage, and divorce, that the system could chew up and swallow by the dozen on a typical weekday morning.

It was the fact that the system was, this morning, operated by Judge Curtis himself that made this prove-up a bit more tense for me than it should have been. Any of the family law district judges could hear a prove-up, and they had worked out a rotating schedule among themselves for doing so. Because I was not a regular for the courthouse prove-up docket any more, I had forgotten that Tuesdays belonged to Stephen Curtis, and I quietly let out a sigh when the court clerk reminded me.

The clerk had built a stack of files to set in front of the judge, in the order in which each attorney had arrived that morning and put his name on the list to have his case proved up. I looked around the courtroom and saw that there were about two dozen lawyers here this morning, and I had been diligent enough to sign in fourth. The only thing more insufferable than coming down here to prove up a case was waiting through 20 bumbling, slow lawyers to prove up their own cases before you, so at least I would avoid that. Or so I thought.

The courtroom observed its ancient rituals (not "ancient" because it was a courtroom in Dallas, where nothing is ancient but is often old, but "ancient" because these rituals had been performed in courtrooms around the Western world for centuries) of a bailiff announcing the arrival of the judge, then the entry of Judge Curtis looking either magisterial or queer in his flowing black robes (depending on whether you knew him or not, I suppose), then the odd but familiar sound of dozens of clothed backsides sliding up and off wooden chairs and pews, then re-seating themselves after Curtis waved the gesture away with an annoyed-sounding "Please be seated." But everyone knew he relished the ceremony, no matter how many times it had been played out over the foregoing decades.

I know the reason for these rituals, and I recognize the importance of a judge maintaining an air of mystery and pomp among the masses, but some judges seemed to think it was done for them personally, and not the court. These are the same judges, like many officeholders in a democracy, who come to think they "own" a certain bench or legislative seat. That way hubris, and often bitter disappointment, lies.

And speaking of hubris, the black-robed and imperious Judge Curtis called the first three cases, never appearing to look up from the papers in front of him, and mumbled the usual sweet legal nothings to the court reporter seated to his left as each supplicant approached him and requested absolution from their marital mistakes. It was when Curtis reached for the next file, glanced at it, and then tucked it underneath the stack, that I knew he was aware of my presence.

Gandhi would have ignored this slight, but then Gandhi never ran for judge in Dallas County, so what did he know? When Curtis called the name of the fourth case and a lawyer and her client stood up and began making their way to the bench, I also stood up and gigged my client, Stan, in his back, propelling him forward.

I wasn't sure, as I approached Judge Curtis in his position several feet above the rest of the courtroom and behind a mammoth wooden construct simply called "the bench," what I would say or do, but it seemed important to me to say or do something. I'm sure it was the testosterone talking.

But before my words came forth, Judge Curtis finally looked up at me and spoke.

"Mr. Spiczek, what a pleasant surprise to see you in a courtroom. I believe you will find, however, that I have not called your case." All Curtis needed was a scythe in his hand to complete his appearance of being the Grim Reaper.

I decided to act surprised.

"Oh, your honor," I said, trying to sound like someone who is only pretending to be sincere, "I apologize. I thought you had called the fourth case, and I know I'm the fourth case this morning because I saw my file placed in the stack in front of you in the fourth position. And your helpful bailiff also told me I would be fourth this morning."

I can only describe the looks Stephen Curtis and I bandied as one of two roosters sizing each other up just before the fight begins. (And I say this with trepidation, having never set foot in a chicken coop, or yard, or wherever it is chickens spend their time before they make their way to the supermarket.) Curtis glared at me. I glared back. I knew that he knew that our "discussion" had nothing to do with the order in which Judge Curtis was calling his docket and everything to do with pride and respect, of the peculiar male variety. If either of us possessed colorful feathers, our plumage would be in full display in front of the onlookers in the courtroom, who were, I could sense, uneasy.

Curtis spoke first.

"Thank you so much, Mr. Spiczek, for your assistance in running my courtroom." Wow, he was pretty good, too, at sounding like someone who was only pretending to be sincere. "Nevertheless, at least through the end of this year, I can handle this job myself, as I have done since before you went to law school."

I had to see it through, now.

"Oh, of course, your honor, absolutely. I was just confused when you called the fourth case this morning, and it wasn't mine, seeing as how I know my case was fourth. But, clearly, if you want to take cases out of order, I'm sure you have your reasons that I wouldn't understand. My client and I will go sit down, then, and wait for you to call us."

And with that, I gave the best "Fuck you" smile I could muster, nodded at a couple of lawyers standing by, and shepherded Stan to a place on the front row of benches. A lady in a flower-print dress, presumably another client waiting to have her case proved up, had to shuffle her bulk a couple of inches to make room for us, and she didn't look too happy about it, either.

Stan looked at me with the wrinkled brow of concern but didn't say anything. I was still sporting my grin, knowing I was being watched.

Curtis called out the next case again, but he stumbled over the name and sounded a bit shaky. There was a moment, when I heard him, that I regretted my verbal challenge; it isn't nice to show up people in their own domain, and it probably isn't prudent, either. Nice, prudent people, though, lead lives of quiet desperation, and by God, it felt good to be loudly desperate. In moderation.

And sure enough, I saw Curtis finish the case he'd called in my place, then I saw the motion of his right hand as it reached toward the bottom of the stack of files and pulled a folder out, putting it on top. This was done furtively, but I was looking for it.

Curtis called out Stan's case number and name, and my client and I approached the bench. I thought Judge Curtis might find a reason to deny Stan his divorce just to get back at me, fixing on some error in the paperwork as an excuse. But no, everything went normally, and Stan gave the correct one and two-word answers to my questions, just as we had rehearsed in the hallway.

As I was turning to walk away from the bench, though, Curtis said, "Mr. Spiczek, may I have a word with you?" He motioned me to walk over to the side of the bench, where four steps led up to his throne, and where no one could hear us.

"Of course," I said, and strolled over, telling Stan to wait for me outside.

I knew this would be ugly, but I didn't expect Curtis' indirect attack.

"Mr. Spiczek," Judge Curtis whispered to me from atop Mount Judiciary, leaning down from his wheeled chair so as to be heard. "I am doing you the courtesy of telling you that I intend to support your opponent in every way allowed me by the Canons of Judicial Conduct."

This was followed by a studied glare. And I mean "studied" because I could just imagine Stephen Curtis sharpening his scowl in a mirror at home.

Trying to look unfazed (and who tries to look fazed, anyway) I responded, "I do appreciate the heads-up, your honor. But I think you'll find the Canons of Judicial Conduct really tie your hands in races that have nothing to do with you." I emphasized the last words.

Curtis' eyes narrowed even more. "You'd be surprised," he said, and turned away from me with a swish of his robe, indicating that our convocation was concluded.

Curtis had used the last refuge of a coward and a verbal bully. He had abused his position of power to threaten me and to have the last word. I swore to myself then that, if I became a judge and sat where he was now sitting, I would never do that. But even as I turned and walked out of the courtroom, avoiding the inquisitive eyes of other attorneys and their clients, I had to wonder whether a younger Stephen Curtis had made a similar vow.

CHAPTER EIGHTEEN

Things are getting ugly," I told Loren that evening over dinner, and I replayed my morning altercation with Judge Curtis. I also told her that when I was leaving the courthouse, Simon Levenstein, a fellow family lawyer and someone with whom I'd clashed in the courtroom over the years, approached me.

"Oh, no, I'd better keep my hand on my wallet," Simon had said, loudly, to make sure that the other family lawyers in the hall around us heard him. "If a judicial candidate comes to the courthouse, you know he's gonna hit you up for a campaign donation, am I right, counselor?"

Simon was the kind of guy who had never mastered the nuances of humor, as in what's funny and what's not. Perhaps he was aware of this himself, thus explaining the insecurity that drove him to pepper his rapid-fire speech with questions seeking verification of what he said.

But, I played along, even though my mood was sour after my confrontation with Judge Curtis.

"Simon," I had said, as loudly as he had spoken, "I do need your money, and I'll be discussing the state of your wallet with you very soon, but not at the courthouse. I think that would be inappropriate."

I pasted a smile on my face. A candidate must kiss a lot of ass, but for God's sake, there has to be a limit. Besides, I doubted Simon would give me very much.

"So how *is* fundraising going?" Loren asked me.

We were eating, with Elizabeth, at Crab Clause, a cheap seafood place started by a former lawyer I know. The name was supposed to be evocative of Bill's past life as a corporate lawyer, but I think it just confused people. It didn't look like Bill was going to make it, but he had put on a brave face as he greeted us at the door. The problem is, people shouldn't go to a restaurant that's in financial trouble, especially a seafood restaurant in Dallas, if you know what I mean. The smell of financial distress permeates the dining room just before other smells waft in, is my theory. This would be our last visit.

"Jeff tells me we're doing just fine. We haven't raised as much as Hildy, but beyond a certain point, more money probably doesn't matter anyway. And it's no surprise that a Republican in this town would raise more money than a Democrat, even if it is at the judicial level," I said.

"Are these the fingers of the crab?" Elizabeth asked, as she stared with wide eyes at a crab claw.

Loren and I exchanged looks.

"Um, not exactly, sweetheart," I said. "It's kind of like when you get chicken fingers. You know, they're not really the chicken's fingers because, well, chickens don't have fingers."

I soft-pedaled it so Elizabeth wouldn't have a sudden moment of carnivorous insight and cause a scene in the restaurant. I thought that the last thing my friend Bill needed was a five-year-old screaming "Oh, gross!" and hurling a crab claw across the room and into the face of one of the few other diners in the joint. That would go better at home.

"Oh," Elizabeth said, reasonably. "Then this is the *body* of the crab." And with that, she went to work sucking out the meat.

It's unsettling, for reasons I haven't, and don't want to, examine, to see my little girl sucking the very marrow from an animal, and calling it the "body of the crab," which sounded an awful lot like the "body of Christ." I probably shouldn't have had the *grande* cappuccino from Starbucks at 2:00 p.m. It was causing me to suffer cognitive dissonance at dinner.

After you've been married for many years, as Loren and I have been, you may experience the phenomenon of thinking something and then hearing your partner actually express the same thought out loud. I've wondered whether this happens because we're so much alike, which is why we married each other in the first place, or whether years of living together are what cause this. Loren was probably wondering the same thing right now.

What she said, though, was "So what if the issue of religion comes up at this candidates forum? It's taking place in a church, after all."

"I don't know," I replied, "What if it does?" I shifted my weight.

"Because of that right there," Loren said. "You get nervous when people talk about religion. So you might want to be prepared for it ahead of time."

Yes, that would be the best way to be prepared, I thought. Ahead of time. Another rule of marital longevity is to avoid giving voice to every smart-ass thought that pops into your head. That's what golf buddies are for.

"I think I'll be fine," I said, trying not to sound testy. That was something I'd been practicing, at Jeff's behest: sounding less testy. I found the effort irritating.

"I think I'd like to be a crab for Halloween," Elizabeth interjected as she swiped her hand across her lips. How must we look to the alien space beings monitoring our planet, which, with our luck, are super-intelligent cows and chickens and crabs? Or, for that matter, how must we look to the cows and chickens and crabs right here on Earth? Like bloodthirsty predators I supposed, even the five-year-olds.

But if you do want an encounter with an alien species, just look into a cat's eyes sometime, and try not to be the first one to break contact. There's something going on in there, and it may not be benign.

Loren was still talking about my perceived difficulty with religion.

"...is all I'm saying," she said.

"Well, sure, I'll take that into consideration," I replied, having no idea what she had just said, which I knew she knew. Elizabeth was now making gestures with her hands and fingers that mimicked a lobster but I think were intended to be a crab. It's a fine distinction to humans but may mean the world to crabs and lobsters.

As we drove home, I felt that enveloping paternalism that can envelop me when I've just had a big meal with some wine, and my wife is beside me and my daughter is nodding off in her booster seat in back. I think this is a timeless sort of feeling and could just as easily have been felt by a man riding a mule with his family after a good day at the market. It makes me feel right with the world, and more in control than I really am. These moments are like bubbles on the surface of water, delicate and precarious.

Resting my left hand lightly on the steering wheel and using my right hand to give Loren's knee a squeeze, I said, "You know, this has been a good experience, running for office, no matter what happens."

"For whom?" Loren asked, and the bubble was burst.

"Well, I guess I meant for me, but has it been that bad for you?"

Loren looked out her side window. "No, but I'll be glad when it's over. You're gone a lot, and you've been pretty obsessed with this race, to the exclusion of pretty much everything else," she said.

Well that didn't sound good. Should I argue? Should I agree? How about I just remove my hand from her knee and put it on the steering wheel. Damn, sometimes all a man wants from his wife is unconditional support in all his endeavors and opinions. Is that too much to ask?

But what if she's right? My blissful feeling was gone for the night. Five years ago, I probably would have argued with Loren, but whether it's age or fatigue (which add up to the same thing), I didn't feel like arguing with her now. In fact, I surrendered by saying she was right, I had devoted most of my energy to this campaign, and I apologized and said it would be over soon, and one way or another, we'd get back to our normal lives. If one listened carefully, the sound of a cracking whip could be heard over the traffic noises, but I told myself I was just choosing my battles wisely.

Loren didn't say much, she just looked out her window. But her body said, "Yeah, right." Her body could be very sarcastic.

Still, we made it home in a state of prickly consonance, which allowed my wife and me to enjoy some energetic lovemaking, and that left us as physically sated as if we'd worked out with heavybags in a gym. This was good, and I think we both slept well. I know I did. Never forget that, no matter how clever and intellectual we think we are, beneath it all (or maybe above it all) we are simply a species of animal we call *homo sapiens*, a type of mammal that needs feeding, shelter, clothing, and sex, not always in that order.

By the time I got to my office the next morning, I felt refreshed and energized, which I thought was a good thing when Carol put through a call to me from Gloria Stapleton. It looked like I would need a good reserve of *bonhomie* for a conversation with the Grim Weeper.

But no, this day's Gloria had energy in her voice. She was direct, forceful, powerful-sounding, even. And she was angry, very angry, with me.

"Mr. Spiczek," Gloria said (and I knew then I was in trouble because those raised from the early 60s on only refer to their contemporaries by surnames when distance is required, such as the distance required to be high pissed at someone), "What the hell did you tell my husband? He suggested yesterday that I should voluntarily check myself in to a psychiatric hospital. I thought you were supposed to keep my confidences. Isn't that part of the ethics of your profession?"

"Gloria," I said, modeling calmness, "I'm not sure what your husband told you, but remember, he may not be the most trustworthy source, and besides, I haven't spoken to him. *That* would be unethical. Maybe you should tell me what he said."

Stephen had called Gloria and told her that his attorney told him that her attorney had said Gloria was on the verge of a nervous breakdown and might have tried to kill herself once already. Reportedly, I had told Samantha that I thought Gloria should be "institutionalized" for her own good and that this would, of course, delay the divorce.

"Gloria, let me interrupt you there a moment," I said. "Did Stephen sound upset with the idea that the divorce might get put off?"

"Yes," she answered. "In fact, I think that's what was really bothering him. He said it wouldn't be fair to Maria to make her wait any longer."

"Oh my God, did he really say that? What did *you* say?"

And I heard an unexpected, and quite wonderful, sound. Gloria Stapleton laughed, something I hadn't heard her do over the course of several hours of conversation. Sure, it was the sharp-edged laugh of vengeance, but it was a start.

"I told him (and now Gloria sounded like she was stifling a giggle) that I felt bad for Maria, and I hated to be so much trouble, but that I really didn't think I was up to a divorce right now. I may have told him that if he wanted to be rid of me so badly, it probably wouldn't be a problem for much longer, one way or another. (Stifled giggle)."

"Oh, Gloria," I said, "you were a bad girl, weren't you?"

"No worse than you were when you made Stephen's lawyer think I had a razor blade raised to my throat."

But Gloria didn't sound angry any more, and we were back on a first-name basis.

"Norman, is this sort of thing ethical?"

I sat back in my desk chair and sighed gently into the phone.

"Ah, ethical," I said. "Yes, I think we stayed on the proper side of the ethical divide. If I had actually told Samantha that you had tried to kill yourself, that would not have been ethical because, as far as I know, it would have been a lie, not to mention a possible violation of attorney-client privilege. But I said no such thing. I told her I was concerned about you, that I thought you were depressed, and that if indeed you did have an emotional...disruption...of some sort, it would probably delay the divorce and possibly cost Stephen extra money in spousal support. And all of those statements were true. I was counting on Stephen's momentum to do the rest."

"Stephen's momentum?" Gloria asked. "What do you mean?"

"I think of it as the *'toro'* approach to the practice of law, like a matador. If you take on a bull head-on, you may get gored. But if you flash something at the bull that he wants, you can lead him where you want him to go. In this case, Stephen, I think, wants a quick divorce at least slightly more than he wants to save money, and we're just helping him get there."

"So you can stab him as he goes by," Gloria said, and this time she didn't stifle her giggle.

There's always been something frightening to me about a vindictive woman. Men only think they have the market cornered on combat. The truth is, women fight, when they do, like they do everything else: practically and without a lot of unproductive bluster. Gloria's zeal was making me nervous.

"Well, I don't know about that," I said. "Maybe it's a higher sort of ethic. I mean, after all, if Stephen hadn't cheated on you, and if he weren't so eager to get out of one marriage and take up another one, he wouldn't be susceptible to my suggestion of your possible mental instability. It's his own covetousness that has done him in, not me."

"Whatever," Gloria said breezily. "I think I can take it from here, Norm."

CHAPTER NINETEEN

Parkview Methodist Church must have been designed and built by the same people who brought us strip shopping centers and drive-through (no, "drive-thru," in modern American usage) banks. It was not quickly recognizable as a church. The stylized cross raised above the one-story red-brick building was made of brushed stainless steel, and looked soulless and industrial, and similar to the logo of a certain national brokerage outfit. Maybe that was the idea: "Have you invested in God yet? Check out our annual returns!" I could envision the ad campaign.

The Sunday afternoon sky was threatening a storm, as fall Sundays often do in North Texas. The heavens here threaten hail and other largish, windborne projectiles, and the Weather Gods make good on the threat often enough to engender fear and loathing from the citizens. Thinking in religious terms today, I thought that perhaps mercurial thunderstorms were our penance for avoiding hurricanes and earthquakes. You know, into every life some random mayhem must intrude. I also didn't like parking my car in the open parking lot.

"Okay, buddy, here we go," Jeff said to me as he, Loren, and I walked into the church. Jeff slapped me hard on the shoulder, leaving off only a pop to my backside with a wet towel to complete the locker room effect.

I wore what I thought of as my "funereal" suit, a solid black Armani that fit me as if it had been poured over my body.

A dark blue shirt with rigid collar, along with a patterned tie that was also rendered in black and dark blue, made me look serious, I thought, in a gangster sort of way. When Loren had seen me come downstairs in this outfit, she had said, "You'll need to smile a lot to counteract that suit. But don't make it too toothy."

I tried out my toothless smile on the first person we encountered upon entering the church's doors. I extended my hand to a lumpy woman in a purple dress with flowers on it (even I knew it was more of a JC Penny spring line than it was fall wear), and said, trying not to reveal too much tooth, "Hi, I'm Norman Spiczek."

The woman put her doughy (and unpleasantly wet, from what I don't know and don't want to know) hand in mine, and said, "Hello, I'm Bertha Stintmueller," which is exactly what it said on Bertha's nametag: "Hello, I'm Bertha Stintmueller." It was one of those plastic nametags, not the temporary paper kind, so I figured Bertha must be a regular here.

I could do this now with little unpleasantness, like swallowing your overcooked, slimy vegetables in one gulp when you're a kid, just to get it over with.

"Bertha," I said, "how nice to meet you. This is my wife, Loren, and my friend and campaign manager, Jeff." Bertha stared at us. She didn't have a tag for this.

"We're here for the candidates forum," said Jeff. "You know, the judicial candidates. The ones running for judge?"

"Oh, yes," said Ms. Stintmueller. "That will take place in the North Narthex, right through there."

"The North Narthex," I repeated. "Wow, do you have more than one narthex? A lot of churches don't, you know."

Bertha stared, then said, "It's the North one, that way." She lifted her floppy arm to point to a hallway.

"Ah, thanks Bertha," I said. "We'll see you in there."

Now she came alive.

"Oh, no, I can't go in there," Bertha said, as if I'd invited her to a strip club. "I have to get home and take my pot roast out of the crockpot. Edgar and his kids are coming over, and then we've got the cousins staying with us. If I don't get home soon, it'll all be ruined." Bertha seemed distressed.

"No, no," I said, as if trying to calm down a knife-wielding maniac in a bank lobby, "that's okay. You should go home and get your pot roast. That's more important, and you don't want to ruin your meal."

"Cause if I don't get it out," Bertha continued, "it gets all stringy and tough. Edgar won't eat it."

"Right," I said, looking at Bertha but moving my feet toward the hallway. Loren and Jeff weren't helping by just standing there, watching this tableau. "You take care now, Bertha." I did my smile thing.

Loren murmured a "nice to meet you" and poked Jeff in his side to get him moving with us. My wife took my hand in hers and whispered, "Go ahead and use your teeth."

"Yeah," Jeff concurred, and then followed with "That was so weird."

I could tell that the long- hallway-like room we were approaching was the North Narthex because a laminated faux-wood sign by the door said "North Narthex," just as the same kind of sign would announce the "Trinity Conference Room" in a roadside Marriot. The carpet was probably somebody's overrun; it was bright red and green, in crisscrossing diamond shapes. It might have been intended for a country club's dining room, and the church got it cheap when the country club lost its financing.

Jeff was doing his job by spotting the nametag of the

church's coordinator for this event, and Jeff walked up to the man in a confident way, smiling with his teeth.

This is what Jeff was good at.

"Mr. Goggins! I'm Jeff Frankel, we spoke on the phone. I'm very pleased to meet you."

"Gavin Goggins," said the alliteratively-named man behind the name tag. "Thank you for coming to our church. And this must be the candidate himself, Mr. Spiczek."

I like any man who pronounces my name correctly on the first try. And after my initial encounter at the church, it was refreshing to meet Gavin. He seemed normal. As introductions were made all around, it turned out that Gavin was an associate minister at the church, which I took to mean an ecclesiastical vice-president of sorts, and he was in charge of the church's "outreach" program. Evidently, Hildy and I were the recipients of today's outreach.

"I hope you didn't have any trouble finding the narthex," Gavin said. "It is sort of tucked away in the back."

"Oh, no," Loren said, who was really good with using her teeth when she smiled. "Ms. Stintmueller showed us the way."

This seemed to cause a stutter in Gavin's body language. "Oh, uh, you met Bertha. Well, wonderful. Um, let me show you where you'll be, Mr. Spiczek." I should have told Gavin he could just call me "Norm," but I kind of liked hearing him say my last name so well.

As Gavin steered me toward the front of the room, I asked him, "By the way, Gavin, is there more than one narthex at your church?"

"No," Gavin said, wrinkling his forehead. "Just the one."

"Hmm. Well, anyway, Jeff already told me the format," I said, "and I'm fine with speaking for a few minutes and then taking a few questions from the audience, if they have any.

This is really a good turnout for this sort of thing." I was distracted when I noticed that Hildy seemed to know several of the people here, judging by how many times she stopped to talk, hug and blow air kisses. "Huh," I murmured.

Gavin followed my eyes and said, "Oh, Ms. Pierce is a frequent visitor to our church. I think she knows some of the other parishioners."

"Does she now?" I said.

"Oh, and by the way, Mr. Spiczek," Gavin said, "when the church's Community Relations Committee last met, it decided to also allow the candidates to address each other directly. I'm sure your campaign manager mentioned that to you."

I shot eye darts at Jeff, but he was busy eating one of the donuts he'd found on a back table, which I think he was supposed to pay for and probably hadn't. No, Jeff had neglected to mention that to me, but I told my new clerical pal Gavin that it would be just fine.

As Hildy made her way to the front like a rock star greeting her fans, Gavin tried to make polite conversation with me.

"So, Mr. Spiczek, do you have a church home?"

"A church home?"

I pictured a wizened old woman, dressed in faded black clothes, creeping around a choir loft after everyone else had left. "Not as such. I think I'm a Unitarian." As if that explained my lack of a "church home."

"Ah," said Gavin, tilting his head back slightly. "They're good people, too, Mr. Spiczek."

"Thanks."

He could stop saying my last name about any time now. Gavin sounded like someone who had taken to heart the old

Reader's Digest suggestion that saying a word repeatedly in a conversation will cause you to "own" it.

Hildy approached me and stuck out her hand to shake, in what I thought was a very showy manner.

"Norman," Hildy said, "isn't this a great turnout? Gavin, Norm and I just want to thank you for arranging this."

I felt like my mother was thanking a playmate for me. ("Norman had a great time at your house, Timmy, didn't you Norman?").

"Yes, of course, Gavin (I guess we're using first names now), I was just thinking how wonderful this is," I said, lamely. "Really. It's great."

Then Hildy gave a little rehearsed-sounding giggle and said, "Besides, the Cowboys are already down 14 in the first quarter, so we certainly aren't missing anything there."

I hate this woman's very essence, I thought.

I was rescued by a guy in his 20s with a full, untrimmed black beard and wearing black jeans and a black T-shirt that read, in white, block letters "Take me away, Calgon!" He smelled a bit gamey as he approached me.

"Hey," he said, "I'm Jason Sanborn. I'm a reporter, I think Jeff told you about me. When you guys are finished, I want to talk to you."

Jason spoke as if Hildy wasn't even standing next to me, which she was. She shifted her weight from one mid-heel to another, then stuck that hand out again, this time to Jason.

"Hello, Jason, I'm Hildegarde Pierce."

"Hey," allowed the taciturn journalist.

He briefly shook Hildy's hand, then he turned sneaker and walked to his seat toward the back of the room. It didn't escape my notice that Hildy reached for a paper napkin in front of her and wiped the palm of the hand Jason had grazed.

Gavin stepped in and said, "Okay, folks, let's get started."

He blew into the microphone a couple of times and asked people to take their seats. Loren gave me a smile. Jeff gave me a thumbs up. Hildy blew an air kiss to a woman in the front row.

"Hello, everyone, and welcome to our humble church. Let us pray," Gavin said, bowing to the microphone.

What? We're praying? No one had said anything about praying. But I lowered my head in unison with the others and listened to Gavin, whose voice had taken on a different tone, like he had God on the phone, and Gavin was fairly intimate with Him.

"God Almighty (it was funny to hear that phrase uttered with reverence and not as a curse after stubbing your toe in the dark, but I suppressed my smile), we want to thank you for allowing us to come together today in your presence. Please be with Norman and Hildegarde (and here Gavin nodded toward each of us, and I wasn't sure if he was introducing us to God or to the audience) as they seek to be elected judge. We thank you for allowing us to live in a country in which we are free to vote for the candidate of our choice, and we take the responsibility that goes along with that right seriously. Please guide us in this matter and grant us wisdom. In Jesus' name, amen." Amen, echoed the crowd.

I noticed that many in the audience had that look on their faces that I remembered from going to church when I was a kid, the look that was especially evident when I'd watch people return to their seats after receiving communion. It was a look of contentment, but it nagged at me because it had a Stepford-wife quality to it as well. If you can see intelligence in a person's eyes, and I think you can, you can also detect vapidness where critical thinking should be. Maybe this is why religion, and the buildings that house it, make me nervous. At a childhood level, which is the foundation, shaky or strong, on which we build our adulthood, maybe I interpreted that look as one not of contentment but of appeasement.

Many people just want peace in their lives, and they'll trade self-awareness for it. And who's to say they're wrong? What had self-awareness done for me? It was tempting to try to put the apple back on the tree, unbitten, but, of course, it can't be done.

"Mr. Spizcek?" Gavin was talking to me, while the audience was quiet. I could tell from his tone that it wasn't the first time he'd spoken. I felt the eyes on me. "Mr. Spiczek, you may go first and give us a brief background on yourself."

"Oh, yes, of course," I said, standing up and approaching the microphone. "I was just thinking about what I wanted to say. While I'm not always successful, I do try to think about what I'm going to say before I say it." My weak attempt at self-deprecating humor met with the nervous nose-laughs from the audience it deserved.

"Well, first," I began, "let me thank you for having us here at your church home (my Reader's Digest moment), which I consider an honor. My name is Norman Spiczek, and I'm a Dallas County native. I've practiced law here for..." I then fell into the same speech I'd given at several other functions just like this one, because it was easier than thinking. I also sensed the audience was bored, which I certainly would have been if I'd been among them, listening to this drivel.

When I finished and sat down, Hildy approached the microphone.

"Thank you for inviting us to speak to you today. As many

of you know," Hildy said, sounding breathless with earnest excitement like a Miss America contestant about to break out in a tap dance for the talent portion of the show, but thanking God for America first, "I have been a frequent visitor to your fine church. I've always enjoyed seeing how other churches worship God, and I often incorporate the things I learn into my own observance. It may seem strange, but I guess it's a nutty hobby of mine."

There were a few appreciative chuckles at Hildy's wild-woman disclosure, although I saw that Jeff was making the universal gagging sign with his finger in his mouth. Loren swatted him.

Hildy continued.

"And maybe that's the real reason I'm running for judge. Like the way I am always looking for new perspectives on how to worship God, I'm also looking for a new way to serve the citizens of Dallas County. I've given you, gladly, almost 20 years of my professional life as an assistant district attorney, prosecuting some of the most horrible 'parents,' if one can even use that term, in child welfare cases, and it's been my privilege to do so. I think it's fine for some lawyers to focus on making money in private practice (and here Hildy nodded toward me, still smiling), but that kind of law just wasn't for me. At the end of each day, I needed to feel like I had given something back, that I'd made some contribution, no matter how modest, to making the place we live just a little better. I believe that, with your help and the guiding hand of God, I can best continue that service to you as a judge in family law cases."

Hildy then went on to detail her background a bit more, managing to work the word "God" in at least four more times. I may have missed a couple of references because I , too, was thinking about God, but more in the line of wondering why God didn't smite her on the spot.

I glanced at Jeff and Loren again. Loren's eyes were closed, and she was pinching the bridge of her nose with her fingers. Jeff was just returning to his seat with another donut. I could see from where I sat that this one had sprinkles on it, and they were shedding onto Jeff's lap and at his feet.

Hildy finished her sermon and sat down.

Gavin took the microphone and said, "As I've explained to the candidates, we will now take questions from the audience, and the candidates may ask each other questions as well."

A hand shot up about halfway down the rows of seats. The hand belonged to a man who had evidently gotten large overnight and hadn't made the requisite wardrobe changes, based on the way his shirt was so tight that it highlighted the rolls of fat rippling down his front and sides, concluding near his belt in a collection pool of girth. Gavin called on him.

"Yeah," said the man, who, by bracing himself with a hand on each side of the chair managed to rise. "I got a question for the Democrat. Are you in favor of gays getting married?"

Without thinking, I shot back, "Sure, why should *they* catch a break?"

A few laughs, but Michelin Man was not among them. With some effort, he had managed to cross his stubby arms across his chest, and he stared at me.

"How do you intend to treat gays and lesbians?" the man persisted.

Here we go. "I intend to treat them like the equal citizens they are, and you should expect no less from a judge. (Fat boy let out a snort). How do *you* think homosexuals should be treated in court?" I asked.

"They violate God's law," the man said. "And God's law is higher than your law."

And with a self-satisfied grunt, he lowered himself back into his chair. I noticed Gavin shifting uncomfortably in his chair and heard a few unhappy murmurs from the audience. Jeff linked his hands and pantomimed the swing of a golf club. Grip and rip.

"No, no," I said, like Atticus Finch. "This man has a right to speak his mind, and I'm glad to listen. To address your question, sir, I've spent my entire professional career learning the intricacies of the laws passed by the Texas Legislature and our Congress, and I find them Byzantine enough. I wouldn't be so arrogant as to say I know what God's laws are and how to apply them. I'm sure God can handle that on his own without my help."

More quickly than I could return to my seat, Hildy stood up and turned toward me.

"Excuse me, Mr. Spizcek, but since we're allowed to address each other, I'd like to follow up on the gentleman's question." I noticed that Jason the reporter was scribbling into his notebook furiously.

"Sure, Ms. Pierce," I said, "fire away."

"Mr. Stringer's question deserves a serious answer. (Curious that she knew the man's name, even though he hadn't said it). Our county and state are under assault from a segment of society that would overthrow traditional family values. These people believe that marriage should be extended to same-sex couples, that homosexuals should be allowed to adopt and provide foster homes to children, all kinds of things. While I also believe that all people should be treated with respect in the courtroom, and they will be in my courtroom, I support traditional family values," Hildy said, even working up the sound of indignation in her voice.

"Excuse me," I interrupted and looked at Gavin. "Is this speech time or question time?"

Before Gavin could reply, Hildy's voice got a bit colder and she turned to me and said, "Here's my question, Mr. Spiczek. Do you intend to overturn the traditional family values this country was built upon?"

There were a few "Yeahs!" from the room, but I also took comfort in a few comments of "Geez" and other sounds of irritation. Those could have been from my wife and friend, but I didn't turn to look.

"Ms. Pierce, if you think a state district judge is in a position to overturn traditional family values, or anything else, you're going to be mighty disappointed in the job you're seeking. The last time I checked," I said, "a trial judge interprets and applies the law, he doesn't make it. Or did you have other plans?"

Jeff made a fist pump.

"Don't lecture me about..." Hildy began but was interrupted by Gavin, who rapidly seized the microphone.

"Perhaps this would be a good time," Gavin said, "to take another question from the audience. Anyone?" Gavin scanned the room.

An attractive woman who appeared to be in her late 50s or early 60s, wearing a dark blue dress, stood up. She looked conservative, and I braced myself.

"Yes," said the woman, speaking firmly and clearly, "I have a question for Ms. Pierce. My adult son is gay, and I love him very much, and I'm proud of him. He has a good job, he's been with the same partner for seven years, they pay their taxes and volunteer in the community. Is it your position that my son shouldn't have the same civil rights as any other American citizen? And if so, do you base that on something Jesus taught? Thank you."

And with that, this lady, my new hero, sat down again, smoothing her dress underneath her as she did so. There was scattered applause in the room, more poignant, I thought, for the contrast to the silence from those not clapping.

Hildy stood behind the microphone and addressed the woman directly.

"Well, of course you're proud of your son, as you should be," Hildy began. "No one should disown their son or daughter because they choose an alternative lifestyle."

The woman, without speaking further, stood up from her chair, made her way to the end of the row, and began walking toward the door. But Hildy continued.

"I understand this is a sensitive issue," Hildy said, "and you and I may have different opinions about it, but I hope we can talk to each other. It would be a shame if people with different opinions lose the ability to communicate." Hildy was speaking to the woman's back as it went through the door and out, into the hallway, and, presumably out of the building.

It could not be said that Hildy wasn't quick on her feet, and at this tense moment, instead of making it worse by continuing to speak, she turned to me and said, "Perhaps you'd like to address the lady's question?"

Standing at the microphone, while Hildy continued to stand next to me, I turned to her and said, "It occurs to me, Ms. Pierce, that the problem we just saw was not one of miscommunication. In fact, I think you communicated all too well how you feel, and in doing so, you echoed the views of many others as well. Too many people in this country have bundled their prejudices and bigotry in a sanitary package and called it 'traditional values.'"

Hildy's lips were pale and thin with anger, but she didn't speak, not yet at least.

"Well," I continued, "I'm all for traditional values. Values like tolerance, privacy, equality under the law, things like that. You know what I mean?"

Before Hildy could answer, as she seemed about ready to do, a woman stood up from the audience and addressed me. "Is abortion one of your 'traditional values,' sir? There are still thousands and thousands of us in this town who won't vote for somebody who favors abortion."

Hildy gave a satisfied look and nodded toward the woman.

"That seems like a fair question, Mr. Spiczek," Hildy said. "Do you have an answer for her?"

"Sure," I replied. "I don't favor abortion. Who the hell does? I do, however, favor choice, so if you're part of the anti-choice crowd, maybe you shouldn't vote for me. On the other hand, a state district judge won't write abortion laws one way or another, so why are we worrying about it?"

"Because people have a right to know where you stand on such an important issue," Hildy replied. She then addressed the audience. "And I'll tell you where I stand. It's very simple. Abortion is murder, and murder is a sin. I don't need a lot of fancy arguments to give you my position."

Several people stood up and applauded Hildy's comment. When the clapping died down, I spoke again. I could feel my face getting hot as anger defeated diplomacy in my brain.

"That statement is not just simple," I said, "it's simpleminded, and, yes, I'm talking to each one of you who are so easily entertained by a 'so-called' conservative politician feeding you a line of bunk. Why don't you ask her this: given that abortion is legal, does this woman intend to discriminate against citizens in her court who exercise their right under the law? And if so, where does she stop? What if she doesn't like someone's political views, or where they work, or what part of town they live in, or their religion? Will she use that against them, too? And by the way, if Hildegarde Pierce is so into her 'traditional values,' why is she unmarried with no children? Did you ever think about that?"

The room grew quiet, and I immediately felt the tension. Jeff put his head in his hands, Loren winced. I'd gone too far. Hildy looked like she was about to cry. To her credit, she rallied.

"How dare you criticize my personal life. This coming from a man who probably hasn't stepped foot in a church until today. You have no right to comment on my integrity about applying the law."

Oops, the advantage had just swung back to me. For a moment I had regretted my comment, but now I was glad I'd said it, and I had more to say.

"Hell yes I do," I replied. "I have more than a right, I have a duty to show people what a hypocrite you are. Frankly, I couldn't care less if you live alone, with a man, with a woman, whatever you want to do, but you're the one lecturing people about the 'correct' way to live. I just won't let you get away with it."

With that, Gavin jumped toward the mike.

"Okay, I think we've heard a good exchange today, and we'll wrap it up now. Please don't forget our building fund drive, and remember to bring your used clothing and personal hygiene items next week."

I turned to speak to Hildy, but she was already making

her way out into the room, zeroing right in on the woman who asked me about abortion. Jeff and Loren approached me.

Jeff put his hand up for a high five, which I returned out of social obligation, like shaking a proffered hand, even though I was embarrassed by the gesture.

"Hot damn, buddy! Sorry, Rev," Jeff said, lowering his head in the direction of Gavin, who was watching us. "You really kicked her ass today. I am proud to be your friend and campaign manager. Of course, you know you can't win in Dallas County talking that kind of shit."

"Of course," I replied.

CHAPTER TWENTY

J ason the reporter stopped me before we left the church and said he had a couple of follow-up questions. I thought it was odd when he asked what church I had attended as a child and whether I still attended a church today. He also asked me if I based my political views on any particular politician, and I said that I did not, unless it was unconscious on my part. Jason seemed kind of charged-up for a guy covering a county judicial race.

Loren was right to be concerned, and I should have listened to her, although it was too late to do anything anyway. She told me that night, as we lay in bed together, that she was concerned about how the day's confrontation with Hildy might look.

"People take their religion very seriously, you know," is how she put it.

I guess when you get into politics, pillow talk becomes a debate.

"Yeah," I said, "but I didn't attack anybody's religion. If anything, I was attacking Hildy's hypocrisy about religion."

"Yes," Loren continued, "I was there, remember? It's not so much what you said, it's how you said it, and where you said it. Being attacked is in the eye of the beholder, isn't it? Sometimes it's just the tone of your voice. You can sound so dismissive, you know."

"Well, that's just ridiculous," I said, realizing as I did so that I'd just fallen into Loren's trap. It's really not fair, I thought, for spouses to set traps for each other. We have too much inside knowledge. It's what makes divorce litigation so vicious, and occasionally profitable.

If Loren's warning had not been enough, the phone call I received at 2:30 in the morning was. The ringing blended right into the dream I was having, as nighttime calls and alarm clocks can do, causing a momentary disorientation as my brain got itself around the idea that the ringing was from the outside world, not my inside world.

I thought I'd taken too long to get to the phone and that the call was already being routed to voicemail, but I picked up the phone anyway. There was no dial tone, so I figured someone must be on the line. Ringing telephones in the middle of the night rarely bring good news.

There was a pause, then quick-fire words in a woman's voice, tumbled together like they'd been rehearsed and someone wanted to get them out before she forgot them, or lost her nerve.

"God will punish you. You and your family will go straight to hell." Click.

"Who is it?" Loren mumbled from somewhere in the covers.

"I have no idea," I said, and I punched the button for Caller ID. The LCD letters said "Number Unavailable." So I dialed in *69 and got a recorded message saying the caller's number had been blocked and couldn't be dialed.

Loren asked what the caller had said. Should I tell her the truth? I tried to edge around it.

"Evidently," I said, "you were right. Someone registering her objection to my comments today, as best I can tell. She said I would go straight to hell."

In not telling Loren that the caller had included my family in her invective, I had made the kind of in-the-moment decision that might be hard to explain later. I hated not being entirely candid with Loren because we always shared everything, but my instinct had made an executive decision for me.

"Oh my God," Loren said, sitting straight up in bed now. "Did it sound threatening?"

"Well, it didn't sound nice," I said. "But it was sweet of her to clear up any confusion I might have had." Loren was not amused. She asked me if I could possibly identify the voice.

"You know, it kind of sounded like that woman we met today when we first walked into the church. That Bertha woman. But I can't be sure, and besides, she didn't even stay for the debate."

"People who make threatening phone calls in the middle of the night don't need firsthand knowledge," Loren said. "Maybe she spoke with someone who was there. You should call the police."

"And tell them what?" I asked. "They won't have anything to go on. And unless it was God on the phone using a voice like Bertha's, I can't say I was directly threatened. It was more of a prediction, delivered in a rude fashion."

Loren was getting worked up, and I tried to reassure her that I would look into it in the morning. She wasn't reassured. In fact, she became angry with me, which really seemed unjust.

"How can you just lie there and act like nothing happened? Anyone who's threatening you is threatening our whole family (ah, there I felt the stab of guilt, like acid reflux). You got us into this whole thing, now you have to do something."

"Like what?" I was trying to sound reasonable and dismissive at once.

"Something," Loren insisted.

"Fine. I will do something. Tomorrow."

And I turned my head on the pillow and closed my eyes. Twenty minutes later I could tell by Loren's breathing that she was asleep. I didn't sleep the rest of the night, and I resented her ability to do so. Why was she mad at me anyway? I'm not the one who made a threatening phone call at two in the morning. Jesus, women could be irrational.

Loren was distant in the morning, speaking sweetly to Elizabeth, not speaking to me at all. I retrieved the morning paper from our driveway in my bathrobe. The paper was damp at one corner where the sprinklers had watered it just around dawn. I opened it carefully so as not to tear it, and saw a blurb on the left-hand side that promised a longer story in an interior section. The headline read: "Candidate for Judge Takes on God's Politics."

Oh, shit.

I waited until Ingrid came by to pick up Elizabeth for school and then showed Loren the headline.

"You were right," I said.

Loren sat down at the kitchen table with her coffee and read the entire article, which I'd already done. If she was angry with me before, she would really be pissed now.

Jason spun the entire church confrontation as the Democratic challenger taking on not just his Republican opponent but right-wing politics, religion, God, and the American way. To my eyes, I sounded like nothing so much as a pompous ass. And I couldn't even claim I was misquoted because Jason had actually gotten my words down accurately, if not always in the full context. There was even a pull-out quote box under the cutline "Would-be Judge Questions Opponent's Personal Values." The pull-out quote was: "If Hildegarde Pierce is so into her 'traditional values,' why is she unmarried with no children?" Oh, God. I didn't like this loudmouthed Norman Spiczek one bit. He was a mean bastard.

Loren calmly read the entire article, pausing only to take a couple of sips of her coffee, once to tighten her bathrobe around her. This was going to be ugly, and I just sat at the table waiting, cradling my own cup of coffee.

Loren finished, folded the paper, took another swig, then looked at me.

"This is good. It's exactly what needed to be said, and I'm proud of you."

"You are?" Where was the trap, I was thinking.

"Yes, I am," my wife said. "Those fundamentalist types are just bullies, and I can't stand bullies. I'm glad you're taking them on."

When my beautiful wife stood to embrace me, and we made ourselves late to our respective offices as we reunited between the rumpled sheets of our bed, I certainly didn't point out that it had not been my intention to take on the fundamentalist Christian movement in this country and fight for tolerance and freedom. I just wanted to be a family law judge in Dallas County, and I wasn't even sure why.

Ah, well, sometimes our destiny is thrust upon us. Who was I to fight destiny?

I was on my way into work when Jeff called on my cell phone.

"Hey, man," he said, chewing on something between words, "you got more coverage than the governor's race this morning."

"Yeah, but I come off sounding like a jerk." I said.

"Well, it was a jerky thing to say," my campaign manager pointed out. "But it got you some press. I also got a call this morning from Hildy's people saying that she would refuse to appear with you at any other functions until you made a public apology to her."

"You're kidding. She really said that?" I asked.

Chew, chew, swallow. "I don't know if she said that, but someone said she said that. Doesn't matter, it's all just tactics. Of *course* she doesn't want to appear with you, you grab all the attention, make her look bad. Hell, Norm, you're a star! On a very small scale, of course. I got a call from a local radio show that wants to talk to you."

Well, what the hell, I thought. I wasn't looking to be cast as the savior of the left, but I would take the role. It might be fun. Before we hung up, Jeff and I agreed to play golf that Friday afternoon.

It was early October, less than a month before the election, and my campaign was getting hotter as the temperatures got cooler. In Dallas, the transition from summer to fall takes place during the State Fair of Texas, which runs from the last few days of September through the first couple of weeks of October. During that stretch of days, the temperature will go from boiling to temperate, maybe with a couple of false starts. It will rain heavily, too, at least for a couple of days and often during the Texas-Oklahoma football game at the Cotton Bowl. This changing of the seasons could be counted on at this time of year with as much certainty as any weather event could be in North Texas.

Loren and I took Elizabeth to the State Fair after school on Friday, taking off from our jobs early to do so, while the grease was still fresh at the corny dog stand, or so Loren reasoned. My yearly trek to Fair Park is good for me, and I don't mean because I eat any item that can be fried. I mean because I see people (I won't say "rub elbows" because I try to avoid physical contact) with people I don't see the rest of the year. At least not in such massive numbers, and...just massiveness.

I play a game in my head in which I try to decide which people in the crowd are carnies and which are just fairgoers. It's like the license-plate game from when I was a kid: there is no beginning, no end, and no purpose, except to pass the time. A couple of years ago, Loren heard me mumbling "Carnie," "Not a Carnie," "Carnie," as we strolled down the midway. When I told her what I was doing, Loren said I was being "snotty." This year, I saw her lips moving, mouthing out "Carnie," "Carnie," "Wanna-be Carnie." That was a new one.

And then, whom should my little eyes spy but Walter Stokely, wearing indecently-cut khaki shorts and a pink Polo shirt stretched tightly over his girth. Black socks, tennis shoes and a wide-brimmed straw hat completed this grotesquery. He had a fried turkey leg in his hand and fried turkey grease on his lips and chin. He saw me as I saw him, and we reluctantly met up in front of the game where you try to throw over-inflated footballs through a hole in a tarp.

"Hello, Walter," I said, gathering my wife and child to my sides and slightly behind me.

"Good afternoon, Mr. Spizcek. This must be the whole Spizcek clan."

I was forced to introduce Loren and Elizabeth to Walter, but at least he swiped his hand over a napkin before he shook Loren's hand. Walter wasn't the type to shake a child's hand, and I was glad he didn't touch my daughter.

"Just enjoying the culinary delights of the Fair, Walter?" I asked.

"It's important, Mr. Spizcek, for one to immerse oneself in cultures and sociologies outside of one's comfort zone occasionally," said Walter, ripping off another chunk of fried turkey with his little yellow-glazed teeth.

"Ah, well, you actually look pretty comfortable, Walter. Take care now." I put a hand each on my wife's and daughter's backs in a herding attempt, but Walter wasn't finished.

He lowered his voice, perhaps so that the man with the tattoo of a snake running across his forehead and who was barking at us to try the football toss for just $5 for three tosses couldn't hear. He might be a Republican spy.

"Mr. Spiczek, one should try to be more careful with one's words about religion in the atmosphere in which we find ourselves. You may not care that your performance last Sunday jeopardizes your own campaign, but there are many other Democratic candidates in this county who would rather not be associated with a heretic."

"You mean I should mealy-mouth the whole God thing like Democrats have been doing for years while they lose? Is that what you mean, Walter? Listen, if it makes you feel any better, I don't go out of my way to insult anybody, but I won't soft-pedal my anger at the Republican (and I turned from Elizabeth's hearing) bullshit either. If that ruffles some feathers, so be it, although I would have hoped those feathers would belong to my opponents, not the people who are supposed to be on my side."

"Daddy," Elizabeth said loudly, "I want to go on the Tilt-A-Whirl! You promised."

Walter leaned down slightly toward Elizabeth and spoke to her. "Just a minute, little girl, your father and I are not through talking."

"Luckily for you, Walter," I said, and I really was clenching my teeth, "we *are* finished. And don't speak to my daughter again."

I turned to Elizabeth and said, with as much haughty dignity as the following words allowed, "We're going to the Tilt-A-Whirl."

And we did. It must have been my irritation with Walter that led me to plant my butt in a plastic seat and allow myself to be strapped in by a 16-year-old ride attendant who didn't even look like a carnie. Normally, I refused to ride anything more dizzying than the tram from the parking lot, and, contrary to Elizabeth's entreaty, I had never promised her that I would ride the "Tilt-A-Whirl." I enjoy neither tilting nor whirling. It made me nauseous just to stand by the gate and wave at Elizabeth as she rode these things. But surely, if Walter saw me stride right onto the Tilt-A-Whirl and take a seat, he would know what kind of a man he was dealing with. Tilt me. Whirl me. Go ahead.

I wanted to throw up 30 seconds into the ride, but gravity and centrifugal force wouldn't allow it. Elizabeth, of course, has no inner ear, and her stomach is detached from the rest of her body, like all 5-year-olds.

"Yippee, Daddy! Isn't this great!" screamed little John Glenn, stretching her fingers skyward as we were slammed forwards, backwards, and sideways, at once.

It would have been unseemly to throw up on my daughter, so I did my best to compress my lips, but the force of the ride pried them open. I suppose I was making a freakish sort of toothy grin which Elizabeth may have mistaken for enthusiasm. I knew the ride would never end because Hell is eternal.

Thinking that bargaining might help, I skipped over promising to be nice and went right for life-changing alteration. If the mechanical parts of this ride would please freeze up, right now, I would assume a new personality, one more pleasing unto the Lord.

"Silly Daddy," Elizabeth was saying, "we can get off now. There's no more spinning."

Elizabeth was wrong about that. The ride had finally stopped, but there was still plenty of spinning.

The ride attendant was standing in front of us.

"Sir, you'll have to exit the ride now. If you want to ride again, you'll have to get in line and get back on."

I steadied myself. "Oh, no. No. Not again. Please. Just let us off."

I walked toward the exit like a sailor coming off three months at sea, leaning on Elizabeth's head until she told me to stop it. There was Loren up ahead. She would make it better, in that way that women who are mothers can do, even if you aren't their child.

But no, God would put my resolution to the test without waiting. Stepping from behind Loren was Walter Stokely, now spooning something thick and yellow from a plastic cup.

"I have found," Walter said to me in his nasally voice, "that the Tilt-And-Whirl can make one quite disoriented."

"It's a Tilt-A-Whirl, Walter, not a Tilt-And-Whirl." Sorry, God, but come on. He's really a jerk. "Have you ever actually ridden it?" I asked.

"No," replied Walter, "one shouldn't subject oneself to such stress beyond a certain age."

With my arm wrapped around Loren and leaning into her a bit heavily, I steered my family away from Walter Stokely. But I turned back and addressed him over my shoulder just as he was shoveling another glob of yellow into his weak mouth.

"Yeah, well, sometimes you gotta take chances in this world, Walter. Risks be damned."

Loren must have noticed my complexion because she whispered, "Are you going to be sick?"

"Oh, yes," I replied, turning back from Walter. "But not here."

CHAPTER TWENTY ONE

When Jeff and I had started our round at North Dallas Country Club, the sky was overcast, but there was no wind, and everything seemed sort of spooky calm. In Texas, this kind of dark-skied lull in the weather was like you knew there was a storm forming just offshore. But we really wanted to play golf.

The good news about the threatening sky is that it kept the less-committed golfers off the course. Jeff and I teed off with no one in front of us and no one pushing us from behind. This is golf the way it was meant to be played, at your own pace, alone, in unsettled weather. Well, alone with a friend.

"Do you think you can use the word 'broad' about a woman without being derogatory?" Jeff asked me on the third hole.

I knew what he was doing. I had just parred the first two holes, the second one with a slider of a putt from about ten feet out, and I was one stroke ahead of Jeff. He had bogied the first hole and parred No. 2. Jeff was talking to me from his cart as we made our way up the third fairway. My drive was long and straight, and I was jazzed about my game so far. Jeff had popped the top on his first health-food beer of the round.

In response to Jeff's question, I said, "When did you commit this *faux pas?*"

"Tuesday. I just told my secretary that her sister was a good-looking broad. Is that such a crime?"

Damn it. I studied my ball and the remaining path to the third green as I approached on foot. I glanced at Jeff, who had pulled his cart up right behind me.

"Would you back up a bit, please? Yeah, I could see where someone wouldn't want her sister referred to as a 'broad.' The word sort of detracts from the 'good-looking' adjective preceding it. It's similar to the 'she's-not-bad-looking-for-a-fat-girl' thing. Back up a little more."

With no practice swing, I made sensuous, soul-affirming contact with my 5-iron and sent the ball gliding into the purplish sky on a beautiful, arcing path to the green, where it plopped down about 15 feet from the hole.

Once again, I turned to Jeff. "Nice try."

"What?" Jeff feigned looking hurt. I knew it was feigning because it was Jeff, and we were on a golf course. Men who call women 'broads' don't get their feelings hurt on the golf course, and if they did, they wouldn't show it.

"You know what I get tired of?" I asked.

Jeff was considering his shot, which would require the negotiation of a large mesquite tree that lay in waiting between Jeff's ball and the green. Jeff didn't respond to my question, but I persevered.

"I get tired of people who talk too much," I said.

"Man, I know what you mean," Jeff said as he stepped up to his ball. "Gwendolyn talks like she's packing a suitcase in a hurry."

Gwendolyn was Jeff's rarely-acknowledged and less-often seen wife. Loren and I had privately questioned her existence.

Jeff swung and hit the ball perfectly, drawing it into the green and landing it just inside mine. He then turned back to me. "You know, just cramming as many words as possible into a small space. And her pace is increasing."

"Maybe she thinks she has to get it all in before she dies," I said. "My daughter said one time that a person can't die if she's talking because dead people don't talk. *Ipso facto*, as long as you're talking, you can't die. Maybe Elizabeth just figured out feminine logic faster than most women do."

"Speaking of feminine logic," Jeff said, parking his cart much closer to the green than allowed by the rules of golf etiquette, "Hildy's strategy right now seems to be to shore up the vote she'll get anyway. She's talked to a different church or blue-haired women's Republican club every day for the last three weeks, sometimes two a day. Do you know how many Republican women's clubs there are in this town?"

"How many?" I asked.

"I have no idea," Jeff said through his grunt as he bent over to mark his ball on the green. "But it's a shitload. That's a lot of tea and cookies."

"Do people still have tea and cookies? Did they ever?" I lined up my putt.

"Republican women in North Dallas do," Jeff said.

I calmly stroked my putt to within a couple of inches of the hole. In our game, that was good enough to pick the ball up without having to putt it again. Except this time.

"You sure that was good?" Jeff asked me.

"Of course it was good," I said. "It was this close." I held my fingers close together.

"Okay, if you say so." Jeff almost put his own putt in, just lipping around the cup.

"Fuck you," I said to Jeff in a friendly way.

"Right back at you."

It's good to have an understanding friend.

"So is there anything we should be doing right now to counteract Hildy?" I asked Jeff.

"You mean short of shooting her? No, not really. Frankly, nobody really cares about judicial races anyway. Both of you are at the mercy of what happens up-ballot. As the country and the county go, so go the down-ballot races. Except yours may have drawn a bit more interest than usual."

We approached the next tee box.

"You're telling me that now?" I asked.

Jeff shrugged and boomed a drive down the middle of the fairway. I also put one on the fairway, about 10 yards short of Jeff's. He looked annoyed as he got in his cart, and he didn't drive slowly next to me as I walked, like he normally does. Jeff acts casual, but he's as competitive as any other lawyer I know.

As Jeff was lining up his second shot, I spoke. I should have hit first, since I was farther out, but Jeff had arrived at his ball quicker.

"So I got a call from my father yesterday. It was kind of strange."

There was no response, just Jeff's shot that landed a couple of feet left of the green.

"Fuck," he said, to himself mostly, "I pulled it."

"What, are you not happy with any shot that doesn't actually hit the pin any more?"

I stood behind my ball and thought about my shot. Jeff spoke.

"So what was so strange about your dad's call?"

"He used the word 'Google.' Repeatedly."

I swung, felt that no-feeling-at-all-feeling of solid contact and watched the ball soar majestically, straight to the green. The ball landed with a "plop" we could hear from over 150 yards away. Beautiful.

"Yeah," I continued, and this time Jeff nudged his cart along beside me, listening and sipping. "He said he had 'Googled' me and ran across the articles about the election. He was kind of giddy about it, the 'Googling.' It was just weird, hearing my old man use words I expect from a 20-year-old."

"Jesus, it's getting windy."

And Jeff was right, the weather was changing as quickly as it can out on the plains. Just from the time we'd left the tee box to get to the green, the wind had picked up and the temperature had fallen a good 10 degrees. Still, we intrepid golfers pushed on.

With a long putt that barely had the one more roll in it necessary to fall into the cup, I got a birdie. Jeff made par, and we were tied.

Now it was a race of golf against the weather, and Jeff was already taking more practice swings than usual and considering his shots with deliberation.

"It doesn't look like we'll get this whole round in," Jeff said on the 14th hole. "Too bad, you're playing pretty well today."

I was getting testy.

"We'll finish," I said.

I swung too hard on a 120-yard approach shot to the green and sliced the ball off to the right and 20 yards past the target. I glared at Jeff as he got back in his cart, hunched over his beer. It was unclear whether he was protecting his beer from flying debris or just trying to stay warm against the gusting north wind.

I gathered myself and remembered to breathe before I plopped a perfect wedge shot onto the green. Now I was feeling it. I was thinking about my six-foot putt for another par when the first streak of lightening lit up the sky to the northwest, tracing its brilliant path against the bank of black clouds. A couple of seconds later came the sound of thunder that rattled our golf clubs in their respective bags. Damn.

I bent over the ball, remembered "straight back and straight through," and rolled the ball to the middle of the cup and in. I let out a breath of relief. Jeff stepped up casually to his ball, took one look at the hole, and calmly sunk his putt, too. Going into the 15th hole, our scores were tied, something that had never happened this far into a round in all the years we'd played golf together.

This was important. I can't explain why or even justify it. If a woman had been present, both of us would probably have made jokes about the situation and downplayed it. But it was just us, and neither of us needed to say anything. I knew that Jeff knew how important this moment was.

And that's when we heard the huge airhorn back at the clubhouse blast its warning across the fairways, tee boxes, and greens of the entire course. The blast lasted a shrieking four or five seconds and echoed for several seconds after that.

To Jeff's credit, he didn't grin as he looked at me and said, "Sorry, buddy, the course is officially closed. We'd better get the hell out of here before we get struck by lightening."

"Since when are you 'Safety Sam?'" I sounded petulant even to myself. "We might as well play our way in. We have to go that way anyway."

We both looked at the sheet of heavy rain that was advancing towards us from the hole we'd just finished, slamming water into the ground so hard that bits of soil were sprouting like explosions from a fighter plane's strafing run.

"Damn it," I yelled toward the sky.

I ran to Jeff's cart and jumped in, one hand clutching the handle of my push cart so I could pull it along from a seated position. Jeff slammed his foot on his cart's accelerator and we took off across two fairways in a shortcut to the clubhouse. Nevertheless, we were soaked through by the time we made it to the parking lot where our cars were parked next to each other, alone on a sea of asphalt. Everyone else with good sense had abandoned the golf course long before us. There may not even have been any staff inside the building at this point.

I was cold, wet, and aggrieved. Just before Jeff lowered himself into his Lincoln, and shouting so as to be heard above the biblical deluge, Jeff said to me.

"Hey, I think that's the best I've seen you play. Grip and rip, man!"

In a male sort of way, Jeff had said more in those two short sentences than some people say in a 30-minute speech. I smiled as I swiped the sleeve of my shirt over my rain-soaked face.

CHAPTER TWENTY TWO

I know now that an election is kind of like a wedding. There's so much life going on around you while you're busy planning for the Big Event.

And while I was planning, otherwise known as campaigning, I realized what a good life I had. It's not so much that I slowed down to smell the roses as that sometimes in the middle of running I would think I smelled something. "What the hell is that smell," I'd ask myself (metaphorically, of course). "Ah, roses. I didn't see that coming." So that was good.

These moments of clarity existed probably because Hildy and I didn't engage in any hand-to-hand combat after the brawl at the church. She may have perceived that it didn't help her campaign to appear brittle and angry, but if so, she was mistaken. It would surely help her for me to appear aggressive and angry, which I perceived that I did when I was around her.

Of course, Hildy didn't go into hiding in the days before the election. She put together an expensive mailer that featured a studio-made shot of her attempting to look glamorous. To her credit, I'm sure she looked glamorous to some people, but not to me. I know *Jeff* thought she looked good.

"Damn," Jeff said to me in a phone call when he'd seen the mailer, "if I'd known our little Hildegarde could look so hot, I'd have worked for *her*."

"Hot?" I repeated. "How can you say she looks hot? She's just standing there in that ridiculous half-light that photographers always use to cover up things, and *she's* doing her best to cover up, too. Notice how she has her arms crossed over her pathetic little breast humps, as if to hide them in shame? I don't think it would take Freud to figure out she's trying to hide her femininity, as if she should worry about that."

There was a pause on the line.

"You know," Jeff said quietly, "election day can't come soon enough. And please don't ever say that in public."

Jeff asked me if I'd read the text inside the brochure, and I admitted that I'd thrown it into my office trash can without reading it. He suggested I fish it out. I told him I'd already thrown a soiled tissue on it.

"You should take a look," Jeff said. "Hildy appears to interview herself, and she asks herself her strengths and weaknesses. Guess what her weakness is?"

"Please don't tell me it's that she cares too much."

"Bingo," replied Jeff. "I quote, 'People have said I need to take more time for myself, and I do try. I'm involved in my church and with a youth group, trying to relax by involvement in my community. That certainly helps, but I just feel like there is so much work to be done in Dallas County that sometimes I feel guilty indulging myself."

For some reason, this last caused me to speak like a teenaged girl in the mall.

"Oh. My. God. She really wrote that?"

"It's right here in fuchsia and white," Jeff said.

"That is so pathetic. So how come we didn't do anything like that? Do we still have time to work up our own mock interview and get it out on slick paper?"

"I would suggest you listen to how crazy you sound," Jeff said to me, "but I'm afraid you might miss the subtle indicators. Look, Hildy's just shoring up her base. This little baby went to all the zip codes in North Dallas. I really don't see it swaying anyone, but it might help get out her vote a little bit."

"What about *my* vote? How do we get *my* vote out?"

Jeff sounded like Ralph Cramden as channeled through Fred Flintstone. "Oh, don't worry, all the atheists and Wiccans will ride their Saabs and broomsticks right to the polls as soon as they open. You've got nothing to worry about."

"I don't think I like your attitude, Mr. Frankel. Aren't you supposed to be on my side?"

Jeff patiently explained, once more, that turnout would depend on the races higher up the ballot, and on the weather, and on other things out of our control. He was convinced that last-minute spending on judicial campaigns was just wasted money and energy. He called it "panic pandering." I wanted to explore it. He said I was panicking. I pointed out that his reasoning seemed circular and self-defining. He said I was panicking. This seemed an awful lot like a conversation I would have with a client.

It's also true that Hildy and I had engaged in some long-distance sniping without ever actually seeing each other. She had said in a one-minute interview on a local radio station that I just didn't seem to respect women very much and maybe I felt threatened. She made it sound like she was sad for me.

In my one minute on the station, I was sad for myself that I actually said, in rebuttal, "But I *love* women, I always have." Jeff tried to call into to the station to pitch me a softball question, but I was already finished. I questioned him later about what he would have said.

"I was going to ask you for examples of women you respect and admire. You know, like your mom and your wife, or Susan B. Anthony" Jeff said.

"Maybe it's just as well that you didn't get through," I replied. "I probably would have frozen. I might have said 'Catwoman.' I always did have a thing for her."

"Who didn't?" Jeff wondered aloud. "Catwoman was probably our generation's test to see if you were gay or not."

"Or Batman and Robin," I said.

"Ooh," Jeff responded. I guess he'd never thought about that.

And that brings me back to the smell of roses. Metaphorically. I don't know that I've ever actually stopped to smell a flower, but sometimes Loren, and now my daughter, will thrust something into my face and demand that I inhale deeply of its odor. There's no guarantee that the object will smell good, either.

As many times as Loren put something pleasantly-scented under my nose are the times she has thrust refrigerator forget-me-nots at me, barking the same command for either occasion: "Smell this!"

My Pavlonian response now is to recoil and hold my breath, awaiting a further clue, like "isn't that great" or "what do you think it used to be?" I don't think a guy would ever do this. Guys respect private space more, don't we? We'd probably say something like, "Hmm..maybe you should smell this. If you want to. I'll set it over here."

The metaphorical roses in my life smelled good, and I won't even get into the predictable corollary of thorns. Sure, we all know about the thorns. The miracle is that things ever go well. As far as I knew, both Loren and I, and Elizabeth, were healthy. Whether it was true or not, we felt that our whole family was still on the ascending side of life's arc, with a future that would be even better than the already-fine past and present.

Sometimes Loren felt apprehensive about our good fortune, expressing something akin to the "due" theory in baseball, perhaps without knowing the proper name for her worry. If a batter has been hitless for several games, this theory holds that he's due for a hit. The reverse is true, as well. And Loren felt that we were due for some bad luck.

That's when I reminded her that we'd had bad fortune in our lives. Her mother had died of cancer way too young, and Elizabeth had never known her. My father and mother divorced when I was six, thus consigning me to a "broken" home, as they say, or said. In other words, I told Loren, if either of us had failed, we would have had the necessary bad breaks in our pasts to use as reasons, and excuses. Trying not to sound like a poster on the apartment wall of a single woman with too many cats, I pointed out that the key to success isn't what happens in your life so much as what you do with it. Of course, the people who are doing well always say that. Maybe the better way to look at it is that, if we didn't deserve our good fortune, we didn't deserve bad fortune, either.

Given Loren's sensibilities, though, I never shared with her a recurring thought I had. Actually, it might have been more like a prayer, and it was probably shameful. Sometimes, when looking at Elizabeth and thinking how much I loved her and how precious she was to me, and knowing all the horrible things that can happen in this world, I would think, "Please, just pass over this one. Don't let her be damaged or hurt. Please." I wasn't proud of this selfish notion, but I wonder if I was alone in it.

So, anyway, why was I doing this thing, taking months out of my life to try to get a job that wouldn't pay as well as the one I had, taking time away from my family to do so, simply traveling well past the limits of my comfort zone? Ah, well, to ask the question is to answer it, right?

The suburban, middle-class kid who moves up a few rungs on the endless ladder of worldly success in America, while still gripping the middle rungs, has one, great fear. It isn't starvation, or poverty, or loneliness. It's boredom. And woe be to the man who asks God to rid him of the affliction of boredom. Better to handle the task yourself.

And if that were true for me, what might the future hold for my daughter? If things continue for Elizabeth on the same path she's followed for her first five years on this earth, the biggest challenges she will have to overcome will involve a friend or two not being nice to her, maybe issues with clothing or having to eat at a restaurant she doesn't particularly like. Knowing that larger hurdles could arise at any time probably doesn't mean anything to her if they never do. So what are parents supposed to do, create hardships for their children just to test them? Would such artificially-constructed challenges count anyway, or would they be more like some corporate retreat where an instructor designs "team-building concepts," or some such garbage?

By the time our society turns to foreign-sounding and poofy words like "ennui" and "angst" to describe our discontent, it may be too late to save ourselves. This occurred to me recently when I turned on the seatwarmers in my car on the way to work. If the Romans had been capable of seatwarmers, the same would have been installed in their chariots on the Tuesday before their decline began. Still, they felt good when your butt was cold.

Even though I argued with Loren, I think I know what she meant. My love for my wife and daughter, and my life in general, is so great and intense, it sometimes feels like pride. I could easily slip into the delusion that I am responsible for all my good fortune, that it is the reward for my virtuosity, and the people with less, deserved less. And you know what goeth just before the fall.

This residual guilt may even explain my politics. It is, after all, easy to vote Democratic in a state, and lately a country, that is primarily Republican. I get the best of both worlds. My conscience is coddled while my pocketbook prospers. Wouldn't it be a real test of my convictions only if, by voting liberal, I actually sacrificed something?

On the other hand, I didn't create the conditions in which I live, I do follow my heart in how I vote, I'm a nice-enough guy, and I don't owe anybody a damn thing. Besides, I am running for office to serve the people of the county in which I live, and that's pretty damn noble, so to hell with anyone who expects more.

Welcome to another day in the conflicted mind of an American liberal lawyer.

Maybe it all comes down to what I told Elizabeth in a conversation when we pulled up to a red light near the house one day. Towards our car came a man with wild, white hair and sunburned skin, teeth missing, clothing in rags. He limped and carried a cardboard sign which bore block letters saying "Vet. Need help. God bless." I reached into the console of my car and gathered up some change, fingered down the power window and dropped the money in his hand. Honestly, I was just hoping he'd move on and not do or say anything inappropriate in front of my daughter, who was strapped into her government-approved booster seat behind me.

"God bless you, sir," is all the man said, nodding and averting his eyes as he did so.

How must this have appeared to a five-year-old raised in comfort and protection, still new to the world? What in her life up to now could have prepared her for the sight she had just seen? Maybe the only things that came close are the fairy tales which she'd heard, with evil witches and curses and random bad fortune seeming to come from the sky.

"Doesn't that man have a home, Daddy?" asked my beautiful, pristine daughter.

"I don't think so, sweetie," I said, and I felt ashamed, I'm not sure why.

"Why doesn't he? How come we have a home and he doesn't?"

"I just don't know, sweetie. We're very lucky, is all. We're just very lucky." I don't think Elizabeth saw me a few seconds later wipe a tear from the corner of my eye as I turned on the radio to fill the silence that I couldn't stand.

And is that all it is, random luck? Maybe. Like everything else about our lives, maybe we just look back at the events leading up to the present, good and bad, and assign a narrative to them after the fact in an effort to give meaning to the meaningless.

I just don't know.

CHAPTER TWENTY THREE

I saw the future again, and this time it was a heart attack. I didn't have a heart attack, not yet, but I felt that one was coming. Specifically, a twinge in my left shoulder ran down my left arm.

So this is what it will feel like, I thought. Even if I have another 25 or 30 years, maybe five, it doesn't matter, does it? Not when you already know what the end will be. I was sitting on my bed at home, Loren, Elizabeth and Ingrid were downstairs, in the kitchen I think, chatting (women "chat," men "talk," men and women together "discuss"). They wouldn't hear me if I were having a heart attack. Perhaps they'd hear the thud my already-dead body would make when it hit the floor above them, but what good would that do me if I weren't able to see the look of horror on their faces when they discovered me and realized how preoccupied they'd been with their chat, as I lay dying? Well, technically I wouldn't "lay dying" because the way I saw it, I'd be dead before I lay. Still.

No, I didn't have a heart attack that night, but I could have. (I think it was gas or heartburn, that particular rehearsal of my demise). But how could I trust my heart any more? Twenty-year-olds don't think every twinge or tremor is their final act. They could be halfway through a major cardiac infarction, or whatever, and it still wouldn't occur to them that this could be serious. But let a man in his 40s feel tired, and Katie bar the fucking door, it's all over.

And my brain, well, it was losing momentum daily. I once prided myself on my ability to remember the slightest detail of a book or movie, or a conversation. Now I could find myself in a grocery store with no idea of why I was there. I mean this by way of example because, actually, I rarely went to the grocery store. My life had become one of delegation, and now not even that. I had people to whom I delegated the task of delegating. When had that happened? I'm not complaining, just noting. I hate whiners, particularly spoiled ones who don't know how good they have it. You know the type.

I couldn't help but wonder, though, exactly when it was that a person's theoretical death passes the point of being described as "tragically young" to "well, he had a good life." I was probably somewhere in between right now, maybe at the "huh, that's too bad" phase.

I should grow something. That seemed like the right thing to do. I would put my hands in the soil and dig up rooted vegetables. Then I couldn't die. People who worked the land lived forever. Their skin looked like shit, but they were really old. I would work the land in my back yard, around the flagstone path leading from the back porch to the driveway. I wonder if I could produce enough vegetables that way to feed my family and have some left over to take to market. I liked that phrase, "take to market." People who were able to say that also lived a long time, with simple clothing and basic values. And they didn't worry about having toothy grins because they didn't grin a lot. They had the kind of contentment you carry deep inside.

And this is all bullshit. I come from a long line of paper pushers who have lived in relative comfort and developed soft hands. There are hundreds of millions of us now, in urban islands all over the planet, and we may be living on borrowed time, but isn't everyone? If nuclear annihilation is in our future, it'll take out the desk jockeys along with the few grizzled, hard-working laborers still left. Within a couple of generations, through social Darwinism, the "salt of the earth" people will once again reign for awhile, and then we'll go soft all over again.

Meanwhile, guys like me look for their challenges in things like elections to public office, where we don't really risk anything significant, except the embarrassment of losing. As usual, my five-year-old daughter helped me put all this in perspective. As I was trying to get her to bed by reading a story and doing all the usual maneuvers necessary to bring her restless body into its sleeping dock, she popped up in bed and looked at me intensely.

"My name changed today," Elizabeth declared.

"It did?" I asked.

"Yep. My name, everything about me changed today. I'm not the Elizabeth you knew."

"Wow," I replied, "I'm kind of sad about that. I really liked that Elizabeth. What happened?"

"I just woke up," she said, "and, pow, I was someone different."

"Hmm...will Elizabeth come back any time?"

My daughter appeared to ponder my question. She looked at the ground. She furrowed her brow.

"I don't know," she said, "maybe. I think if you give me some hot chocolate, it might bring your daughter back."

I let air out of my mouth like I was being deflated. "Hot chocolate, huh? That's a tough one. I mean, I want Elizabeth back, but hot chocolate is pretty valuable stuff. You can't just be throwing hot chocolate around every time someone disappears. Maybe you should tell me what happened to Elizabeth before I say whether I can give you hot chocolate."

"Well, Dad, sometimes people just change. They don't always know the reason, it's just that they want to do something different. And then, maybe they want to come back to their families, and if you drink hot chocolate with someone from your family, well, you can come back."

Now I was the one who pondered, holding my chin in my hand.

"You know, sweetheart, that makes a lot of sense. I think you're on to something. Let's go have some hot chocolate."

And we did. We went to the kitchen, turned on the overhead lights, and I made some hot chocolate, meaning I boiled some hot water and poured it over two coffee cups of premixed powder. At Elizabeth's urging, I put some miniature marshmallows in the cups because "it wouldn't be the right kind of hot chocolate without them."

Loren walked in on us and said, "I thought you were putting Elizabeth to bed."

"Ah, well, you see, that's the problem," I said. "This may look like Elizabeth, but it isn't. She's someone else, and we're trying to bring Elizabeth back by drinking some hot chocolate together."

Parents of precocious five-year-olds learn to manage situations like this one.

"I see," said Loren, taking a seat at the table. "I hope Elizabeth comes back soon. We've bought a lot of clothing for her, and then there's all her toys. Another child may not like them as much as she does."

For some reason, this caused Elizabeth to crack up.

"Oh, Mom, I'm back. I just had to be someone different for awhile, but I never really left. Dad knew it was me all along, didn't you, Dad?"

I smiled at her. "Well, I was hoping."

And so Loren and I welcomed our daughter home, finished our hot chocolate, and went to bed. I felt the contentment of a family man when he lays his head on his pillow, knowing that his wife and child are safely in their beds, the doors are locked, and all is well.

CHAPTER TWENTY FOUR

I could hear the excitement in Jeff's voice on my cell phone the next morning, as I aimed my car toward work along my well-traveled path. People say that we'll own automated cars in the future that will do the driving for us, but for those of us with morning commutes, it won't be a big change. Our minds slip into autopilot anyway as we roll down the same highways and city streets, not really seeing what's out there any more. With a cell phone pressed to my ear, King Kong could be attacking the 55-story Fountain Place building downtown, and I probably wouldn't notice as I drove by.

The election was two weeks away, and when I saw on my phone's caller ID that it was Jeff, I thought that perhaps he'd found another political event for me to squeeze in, perhaps the Garland Area Rally and Big Action Group Extravaganza, otherwise known as "GARBAGE." Or had I already attended that? I think I had, and there were about a dozen people there, and probably only six of them were registered voters, including this year's GARBAGE princess, Cheyenne Something-or-Other. I was getting a little better at remembering names, but not much.

"What's up?" I asked Jeff, as I drove by the, I think, King Kong-less Fountain Place building.

"Something big," he said.

"As big as King Kong?"

"What?" Jeff asked, sounding irritated.

"Nothing. Go ahead."

"I just got a call," Jeff said, "from someone who knew Hildy when she was 20 years old. Evidently, he doesn't particularly like Hildy, and he wanted to tell me about it."

"Really? I take it she wasn't having sex then either, and he's still pissed about it."

"Uh, not exactly." Jeff chuckled. "Actually, it seems our little Hildy was a bad girl in college. In fact, she got herself knocked up by this guy, and she got an abortion against this guy's wishes. He says he's got a letter written by Hildy at the time admitting what she did, and he's sending me a copy."

"Jesus," I said. King Kong and Godzilla could have been fighting each other right next to my car, and I wouldn't have noticed. "Hildy got an abortion? What a fucking hypocrite she is. I can't believe it."

"Yeah," Jeff said, "when you can't rely on your opponents' integrity, where are we as a society? But you know what this means, don't you? This means the election is yours, man. Her Jesus-freak base will drop Hildy like a fuckin' Kennedy. There's no way she can recover this close to the election."

"So how's this guy gonna use this information?" I asked Jeff. "How will he get it out there?"

"Drink some more coffee, man. He's already used the information by telling *us*. That's how he plans to use it. And he doesn't want us to identify him, either. He says it's burned him up all these years how Hildy unilaterally decided to 'kill their baby,' as he says. Now he's married with kids, and he doesn't want to get mixed up in it. So, what do you want to do?"

I was about to pull into my building's underground parking garage and lose cell contact. "I'm going to think about it," I said.

Just as the line went to static, I heard Jeff say, "I thought that's what you'd say."

I was in a daze as I parked my car and took the elevator to my floor. I said good morning to Carol absentmindedly, and she said that Gloria Stapleton had called and wanted me to call her back as soon as I got in.

"Uh huh," I mumbled to Carol as she handed me the message slip.

I walked to my office, sat down, and picked up the phone. I called Loren at Neiman Marcus and had the good fortune to find her at her desk. More often than not, I had to leave a message for her on voicemail, and we'd play phone tag the rest of the day.

I told Loren that I'd received a call from Jeff, and after some prelude told her the news. I'm not sure why it is that when we have something big to tell each other, we seem to play games about getting to the point. Maybe humans are just natural storytellers, and we know intuitively not to lead with the punch line. We also like to be the bearers of news, which is what makes gossip so much fun. Gossip has a bad name, but have you ever noticed that a lot of it is true? It's the most democratic line of communication and information.

Loren reacted more strongly than I had anticipated.

"What a bitch! What a two-faced, evil little bitch. I can't believe she can stand up there and preach to everyone about how they should live their lives like she's God's own ambassador and then do whatever she wants to in secret. I am so sick of people like her. Why do they think they can just..."

"Well," I interrupted, "she was young, and knowing Hildy, she probably regrets it. It may be that she's become who she is because of getting an abortion, you know, like a self-penance."

"Well that's just bullshit," my usually live-and-let-live Californian wife said, vehemently. "If she'd confine herself to *self*-penance, that would be fine, but she doesn't. She's just become one of those Jesus-y nuts who want to tell everyone else what's right and wrong. Who the hell is she to lecture anybody?" my wife lectured.

"I know, I know. I think the same thing."

"Well, on the positive side, this little revelation will sink her, don't you think? I mean, it may not cause her disciples to vote for you, but at least they won't come out of from under their rocks to vote for her either."

"Yeah," I agreed. "That's what Jeff thinks, too, and I think he's right. But what do you think it will do to Hildy? I mean, you know, personally?"

"It might force her to grow up and be a better person," Loren said. Then she paused. "Oh, I don't know, maybe it'll just make her even more bitter and self-righteous. Whatever." Loren's voice was losing its enthusiasm. "What do you think you're going to do?"

"I think I'm going to talk to Hildy. I think I'm going to meet with her today, and talk to her directly." I had just decided upon this as my next step.

"Do you think you should do that?" Loren asked. "I mean, are you going to ask her to drop out of the race if she doesn't want you to use this information, or what?"

Wow, it's amazing how quickly my non-political wife had become James Carville and Karl Rove all wrapped into one beautiful, blonde package. Kind of creepy, actually. It could change the shape of her face if she weren't careful. Look what happened to those two guys.

I told Loren I'd talk to her later, and I called Hildy at the DA's office. Her secretary answered the phone and couldn't hide the surprise in her voice when I told her who I was. I felt like I was about to be brushed off.

"Please tell Ms. Pierce that it's very important I speak with her. I need to talk to her immediately, and she'll want to hear what I have to say." It was hard to say that and not sound like I was repeating lines from a movie. Maybe I was.

At least four full minutes passed, minutes during which I imagined that Hildy was debating, maybe with herself, maybe with a colleague, about whether she should take my call. Finally, there was an electronic click, and Hildy came on the line.

"Norman," she said, all business. "To what do I owe the pleasure of this call?" Before I could answer, Hildy added, "You know I can't discuss the race during business hours."

I knew that rule hadn't stopped her before, but now was not the time to quibble. When I was ready to hurt Hildy's campaign, I could do far worse than turn up some minor ethical violation. One can only be truly magnanimous when one has the upper hand, as Walter Stokely might say, if he'd thought of it first.

"Hildy, we need to meet today, maybe at lunch. If you have something else, you should cancel it."

"Excuse me?" In her irritation with me, Hildy had taken on a teenage vernacular. "Would you like to start again?"

"No," I said, in a flat tone of voice. "You will want to meet with me, today." As some concession, I added, "Where would you be comfortable talking?"

"I have no intention of meeting you with you, Norman, whatever you're up to, if you don't explain yourself."

"Hildy, I couldn't care less if you meet with me or not, but later, you'll wish you had. If it helps, think about some things you might have done in college that you wouldn't want anyone to know about, and then tell me where you want to meet. I have noon to 1:30 open."

Pause. "If you're threatening or trying to blackmail me, Norman Spiczek, you're dead meat."

"Hildy, when people want to sound dangerous these days, they don't say 'dead meat.' That's way out. And no, I wouldn't call you at the DA's office to threaten you. But *somebody* seems to be threatening you, and that's what I want to talk to you about. So where do you want to meet?"

Another pause. "Meet me at the Sky Club downtown at noon. I'll call ahead and get a private room for us."

"Fine," I said. "I'll see you there."

The Sky Club was a private dining club on the top floor of the tallest building in Downtown Dallas, with floor to ceiling windows offering a panoramic view of the city, from the wealthy suburbs in the far north with postcard grass to the rotting frame houses resting on reddish dirt in the far south. On the rare clear day, you could see Downtown Fort Worth to the west. I was surprised that Hildy was a member, but then I figured the membership probably belonged to someone in her family.

Today was not a clear day, so there would be no Fort Worth viewing. While I sat in my office, the sky reflected my mood by clouding over, getting darker and, well, can the sky get pensive? If so, the sky was pensive. It wasn't raining yet, but it may as well for the gloom in the air. Really, though, this kind of weather, once I got over my anxiety about the golf course puddling up, gave me energy. Fall and winter weather awakens my mind in a way that a slow, hot summer day never does.

I had plenty of work to do, including returning phone calls from clients and opposing lawyers, but I couldn't concentrate. Instead, I paced around my office, looked out the window at the cars below and the dark clouds above, and thought about what I would say to Hildy. Unusually, for me, I still hadn't rehearsed any lines by the time I left. I grabbed an umbrella and decided to walk the six blocks to the building housing the Sky Club.

Bad decision. I had no sooner walked from beneath the protective eaves of my own building when the skies opened. And when you're downtown and bad weather arrives, it's exacerbated by winds created by the canyons of streets between tall buildings, meaning that enough rain blows sideways, under an umbrella, to render the umbrella fairly useless. Actually, worse than useless, because inevitably your umbrella gets crosswise in the wind and serves to pull you onto the street and in front of an onrushing bus if you persist in using it. I'm surprised there aren't more umbrella-induced bus crushings. So, I folded the damn thing up and ran.

Now I was bathing my wool suit in water from all directions. My feet splashed water up my pant legs as I ran, water fell from above, and the wind blew it from the side. Think of running through a car wash in a suit and tie. Think of the golf courses flooding. That's what I was thinking.

When I stepped into the lobby of the Big State Oil Building, otherwise known as the Petroleum Palace, my Ferragamos squeaked as I walked. I shook myself like a dog, causing passersby to make a wide detour around me. I felt like a well-dressed homeless person. I entered an elevator and punched the button for the top floor. My fellow passengers squeezed into the opposite corner from where I stood, scanning me that way people on elevators do by keeping their heads down but casting their eyes up.

I was alone on the elevator by the time it reached the 71st floor. A puddle of water at my feet had darkened the carpet. I squished toward the walnut block hostess stand of the Sky Club. A woman the color of coffee with just a bit of half-and-half (not milk) didn't bother with the head-downcast-but-eyes-uplifted scan. She gave me the full-body once-over, and then said the stupidest thing.

"Is it raining outside?" she asked.

I said what I had to say. "No," I said. "I'm here to meet Hildegard Pierce. I believe she reserved a private room for us." Why did I feel like Benjamin Braddock in *The Graduate*?

The Nubian sentry glanced at her reservation book, ready to tell me that I must have the wrong place, when she saw the entry.

"Oh, yes, of course," she said. "The room is reserved to Mr. Harold Pierce's account. He's Ms. Pierce's father. Do you know Mr. Pierce?"

"Absolutely," I said, still dripping, and not just with sarcasm. "We used to pick up hookers in Tijuana together."

"Heh," was the fake laugh I got from Sade the Hostess. She began gliding down a hall, which I took to mean I should follow her. I didn't glide, I squeaked and slogged. She reached a door to an inner room and motioned for me to enter.

"Ms. Pierce is waiting for you in the Vista Room. Be careful in Mexico." The hostess must have worked on that condescending look in a mirror.

"Oh, I'm afraid it's too late, but thanks." I wiped my hand on the front of my pants, then stuck it out to her to shake. Given the constrictions of society and her job, she had no choice but to take it. I feel sure she went straight to the restroom after I entered the room.

Hildegarde sat at one end of a table for six, East and North Dallas spread out behind her in the windows. All the world, from the Vista Room, was grey to black, and wet.

Hildy stood up and said, simply, "Norman. I see you found your way."

"Not without some difficulty in getting past security," I said, nodding in the direction of the departed hostess/ gatekeeper, "but yes." Hildy made no comment about my soaked condition, which was okay with me as I didn't want to make small talk either.

"You must have some big news," Hildy said. "You were very secretive on the phone earlier. Should I be worried?" Hildy tried to smile, but it didn't come naturally to her bony face. It wasn't toothy, it was…strained, I think. Whatever it was, it would soon disappear altogether.

Just as I was about to dump the news on Hildy, with no further preamble, a uniformed waitress barged into the room. She wore all white and would have looked more like a surgeon than a food server, if it weren't for the 60s-thin black tie around her neck. So, a retro surgeon, perhaps.

"Good afternoon, I'm Mandy," Doctor Waitress said to us. "I'll be your server today. May I get you started with something to drink? Some iced tea?"

When in doubt in Texas, mention iced tea. If in the South, ask whether you want it "sweetened" or "unsweetened." In Texas, which, despite frequent misunderstandings, is not part of the South, people prefer to sweeten their own tea, and this question is not asked.

I wanted to head off Mandy and prevent further interruption, so I glanced at the menu in front of me and said I would like to go ahead and order my lunch. I could see that Mandy was put off by this breach of procedure, but she remained perky and acquiesced. This required Hildy to order as well, which she did.

"And how about you, sir? Would you like to try our delicious golden salmon?" The kitchen must be lousy with salmon they're trying to offload.

"No," I said. "I'll have the tomato soup and the Rueben, please."

"You want the oven-roasted tomato bisque and the old-style New York-inspired Reuben?" Mandy asked.

I could see that she had her pen poised to write down my order but had not yet done so. She looked like nothing so much as an "old-style" school marm who could wait all day until I gave the correct answer.

"Yes," I said, trying to temper the irritation in my voice, but not with much effort, "the tomato soup and Reuben."

Still, Mandy the Pedant wouldn't write.

She said, irritation creeping into her own voice, "The oven-roasted tomato bisque and old-style New York-inspired Reuben, right?"

I handed my menu to Mandy and said, "Mandy, I'm not going to use all the adjectives. I've just had enough of doing that, okay? Do you have more than one kind of tomato soup and Reuben sandwich on the menu? Should I point to which ones I mean?"

"No, sir," Mandy said, all briskness and business now.

As our waitress left the room, Hildy really did smile now, but it wasn't a pleasant smile.

"You must be very confident that restaurant employees don't spit in your food," she said.

"Actually, I'd never thought of it," I said, shaking out my suit jacket as I hung it on the back of an empty chair.

"Perhaps you should."

"So, you're probably wondering why I called this little meeting," I said.

"What I'm wondering is why I showed up," Hildy replied. "I really don't trust you, and it's not as if you're trying to help me."

I chomped an end off a stale bread stick.

"No," I said, chewing loudly and waving my stick of bread for emphasis. "You shouldn't trust me. And that's not why you're here. You're here because you think I might have heard something damaging about you, and you want to know what it is. And you're right. I have heard something damaging. The funny thing is, this same thing wouldn't be damaging to a lot of people, but it is to you."

Hildy primly crossed her hands on the table in front of her and said, "I take it you heard about my abortion when I was in college, and you plan to use it against me if I don't drop out of the race. Correct?"

I set down my bread stick.

"Damn," I said, "you sure do have a way of stealing a guy's thunder. And what if that weren't it? You would have just revealed information to me in a very careless way."

A busboy came into the room to refill our water glasses, but neither of us had taken a drink from them. He circled nervously, pitcher in hand, and retreated. I guess that when filling water glasses is your appointed task, even if you don't really like to do it, you feel cheated if you can't fulfill your mission. Hildy resumed speaking.

"A certain 'anonymous' threatening phone message at my office tipped me off. That asshole of an ex-boyfriend thinks I don't remember the sound of his voice."

I'd never heard Hildy use even the mildest profanity, so now I knew we were letting our guards down.

Hildy, probably unconsciously, was assuming her prosecutorial tone and stance, as she leaned forward in her chair and stared at me without blinking.

"I thought you were pro-abortion, Norm. Why would you raise a stink about a woman exercising her choice? Wouldn't that be hypocritical?"

"That was a stupid thing to say, Hildy," I replied. Hildy flinched when I said "stupid" but otherwise didn't respond.

I continued. "Whatever compassion I might have felt for you just disappeared. But let me set things straight for you. I don't personally know of anyone who is *pro-abortion*, but a majority of Americans *are* pro-choice. Ultimately, though, that has nothing to do with your predicament. *Your* problem is that in your public life you are so hard-line about denying women the right to do what you did. So your problem isn't that you had an abortion, it's that you are an immoral, nasty hypocrite. And you just used one of the oldest tricks in the lawyer's bag which is to accuse your opponent of doing what you're doing, before your opponent gets off the first volley. And if you think that will work for you when this comes out in public, you're sadly mistaken. Even your most moronic lemming-like supporters won't forgive you for this one, even if, or maybe especially because, many of them have had abortions, too. Maybe you just serve as an uncomfortable reminder, know what I mean?"

I had gotten so wound up that I had to pause for breath and to let my blood pressure subside.

Hildy took a new tack. I could tell she was nervous. I could tell that her brain was spinning, trying to think of an angle that would work with me. She was approaching this like an argument in court, assuming that I was the type who would be won over with logic more than emotion. In that, she was right.

Hildy sipped from her as-yet-untouched water glass and dabbed at her mouth with her napkin.

"Norm, you're so bitter and angry. Why is that?"

"Another trick of the courtroom. When you're scrambling, buy time with a question, and attack your opponent to draw attention away from yourself."

I could tell by the way Hildy averted her stare for a moment that I'd hit true.

"But I'll answer," I continued. "I get bitter and angry with people like you who are so arrogant and unfeeling that not only do you deny those less fortunate than yourselves the opportunities and choices that *you* have, you actually justify it with your politics and your religion, which, by the way, amount to the same thing. There's nothing conservative about your type. You don't conserve anything. You destroy, and horde, and divide. Maybe the only thing unfair to you about my anger and bitterness is that I'm attacking you personally for the sins of the entire far right-wing. On the other hand, as best I can tell, you're one of them, so maybe I'm not being unfair."

Just then, Mandy the Miffed Waitress re-entered the room, bearing a tray with our food on it. I'm sure she had heard some, if not all, of my last diatribe, but she went about the business of placing before us our plates and glasses with silent efficiency. In fact, Mandy had swung so far away from her initial perkiness that she didn't even ask us if there was anything else she could get us. She simply slipped out the door without looking back.

In that way that some conversations have of falling into an unacknowledged but recognized rhythym, Hildy and I both knew it was her turn to speak.

"And what about you, Norm? Are you so pure and holier-than-thou that you don't have anything in your past that you would rather not be publicly exposed?"

"If you mean did I drink too much and have wanton, irresponsible sex, yep, I did, but I never claimed otherwise. I've never said that I was 'holier-than-thou,' as you put it. And now you're trying the trick of threatening the one who poses a threat to you."

Hildy looked more relaxed now, and it pissed me off to see her act like she was back in control. I liked it better when she was nervous.

"Well, Norman," she said, taking another sip of water, "since you are so keen on pointing out my rhetorical tricks, let me point out that you didn't answer my last question. You evaded it. Of course you have some secret that you'd rather keep secret, and while I would rather not, I will find it and use it against you if you do the same to me. Don't think for a second that I won't go down without a fight."

Hildy calmly cut her chicken breast to show how composed she was now, so I took a bite of my overnamed sandwich. It tasted like cardboard, which made me even happier that I had not used all the effusive adjectives for it.

"You know, Hildy, you raise a good point. I didn't answer your question, and there probably are some things that I would rather not talk about on the campaign trail."

I deliberately spoke around a mouthful of my sandwich.

"Still, though," I said, "you know how it is. People expect bad behavior from liberals like me, right? The people who support me would vote for me even if you showed that I was a cocaine-using, degenerate, tax cheat, which, sadly, I never have been. Hell, I might pick up some votes. But you, Hildy, you have a lot to lose."

I took another bite of cardboard sandwich so I could talk around it, and then continued.

"For your people, some of them will be upset that you had an abortion, but most of them will just be pissed at your bad taste in getting exposed. They won't vote for a Godless devil like me, but they won't vote for you, either. They'll just skip over our insignificant little race and move on to the other theocrats whom they want to see running this state and this country. And not only will you lose this judicial race, your position at the DA's office might be in some jeopardy, too. After all, if I remember correctly, the DA, your boss, fancies himself as God's man at the courthouse. Right?"

I took another big bite, but I had to swig some water, too, just to keep from choking.

Hildy was shaken again. She had stopped eating and was looking down at her lap. I swear to God, if she started crying, it would just make me even more vicious. But she didn't. She looked like she wanted to, but I'm sure she would rather have died than cry in front of me. Instead, Hildy took a deep breath, and willed herself to look me in the eye again.

"Why would you do that, Norm? Do you want to be a judge so badly that you would try to destroy another human being to get what you want? Or is that you just want to win, that winning means so much to you that you'd sell your soul to do it? Would your family be proud of you? Could you be proud of yourself?"

I swallowed, with difficulty, the bit of sandwich. I could have chewed it for another five minutes, to little effect. I wasn't about to let up on Hildegarde Pierce now.

"Wow, Hildy, you must have exhausted your bag of tricks if you're resorting to shame so quickly." Hildy rolled her eyes and tossed her hair back.

"No, Hildy, I won't reveal your dirty little secret. But it isn't because of anything you've said here today. In fact, it's in spite of it. I despise your kind of political thinking. There's not much that I would enjoy more than seeing you twist in the wind, or maybe the better cliché would be 'hoisted by your own petard,' but I've never been sure what a 'petard' is, so I don't use that one. You absolutely deserve it."

Hildy started to interrupt, but I spoke over her.

"And it isn't because I have pity for you that I won't expose you. I don't. I'm not even that nice. I'll keep quiet for my sake, nor yours. I have no doubt that if you ever did have damaging information about me, you'd use it without a second thought. You'd justify it by saying it was for the greater good, maybe even some bullshit about 'hating the sin but loving the sinner.' The problem is, if I act like you, then I'm no better than you. And by the way, I'm not even sure I fully believe that. There are some times in life when the ethical thing is to act immorally for the greater good, but you're right that an election for Dallas County District Judge isn't one of them."

I got up from the table, threw a $20 bill down to cover my lunch (which it probably didn't at this place), and headed for the door. Hildy didn't stand up when she spoke.

"I hope you've enjoyed your little moment of drama, Norman. Don't expect me to thank you," she said.

"Please don't."

CHAPTER TWENTY FIVE

As I've done all my life, I later reviewed the words I used in my meeting with Hildy and sharpened them. I could have said *this*, or I should have said *that*. The danger I've encountered in this indulgence is that sometimes I forget what I really did say.

I called Loren as soon as I got back to my office, but I got her voice mail at Neiman's. She was probably out on the sales floor or locked in one of her never-ending meetings. So, wondering if it was a breach of marital etiquette, I called Jeff before I'd actually spoken with Loren. Doesn't a voice mail count as an attempt? It seems like that should be good enough, but I'm often the last to know.

"What's the scoop?" Jeff asked without preface.

For some reason, I played coy.

"It was raining like a son of a bitch this morning," I said.

"No shit, Willard Scott. What happened with Hildy?"

So I recounted my meeting with Hildy to Jeff, making only a couple of minor variations to the actual transcript. For example, I didn't think it was important to discuss the strange exchange I'd had with the waitress. I suspected that it didn't make me look good. (Don't be so judgmental: you've done this, too).

Jeff was uncharacteristically silent as I spun the tale, until I finished.

"So you let her off the hook, is what you're saying."

"That's true," I admitted, waiting for the reprimand.

There was quiet on the line for a moment, then Jeff spoke again.

"Good. That was the right thing to do. It may cost us the election, but it was the right thing to do. And if she does win, and I have to appear in her court, she won't mess with me because she'll know I have something on her."

"Always looking on the bright side, aren't you, Mr. Frankel?" I said.

"Just thinking like a lawyer," Jeff said, "whether the side is bright or dark."

This reminded me of something said to me by the senior partner of the first law firm I'd worked for when I became a lawyer. Jim Spence told me that the primary function of law school was not to teach you the law but to teach you how to "think like a lawyer." I'd since learned the quote was not original to him, but it had turned out to be true. While laws come and go, critical thinking is forever.

I needed a bit more emotional confirmation from Jeff before I let him off the line. He agreed that Hildy would probably use similar information against me without hesitation, and that she wouldn't change her ways because of this incident. But it was still the right thing to do and proved that I was a better person than her.

Feeling like a kid cutting class in high school, I left my office early. It would be too strange to go home at this hour, and, besides, I didn't want to have a conversation with anyone, which I would be forced to do with Ingrid and Elizabeth back at the house. Better to surround myself with strangers whom I wouldn't be expected to address. This is how modern Americans remain anonymous in big cities.

So I indulged that most modern of American habits and went to a Starbucks.

You can find one on just about any block north of the Trinity River, but good luck finding one in South Dallas. The part of town south of the river is still neglected by most large businesses and most of the city's political establishment, even though the topography there is more interesting, with hills and trees and wild areas.

One of the unintended, and unexpected, consequences of running for judge has been the number of times I've foraged across the river to speak to civic organizations in hopes of picking up some votes. It always strikes me that I feel far more comfortable, and at home, in the better parts of other towns than in the poorer parts of my own. While hanging around North Dallas or University Park, I can pretend that I'm a rebel because of my political views, but in South Dallas, I'm just another middle-aged white guy in a nice car, there for a quick visit and a quicker escape.

I'm probably supposed to feel guilty about that, but I don't. The personal guilt of white liberals has always struck me as pathetic and useless, as is guilt of any kind, for that matter. Shame, now that's another thing altogether. Guilt is debilitating, but shame has its uses.

But I felt neither guilt nor shame as I pulled up in front of the Starbucks in one of my favorite outdoor North Dallas "shopping villages." I felt a sense of relief, like people used to feel, and maybe still do, on a less-healthy scale when they spotted a McDonalds on the Great American Highway. I wasn't just addicted to the coffee. I was addicted to the clean smell, the neat displays, and the predictability of the menus. That my barista had an eyebrow piercing lent a dangerous and exciting undertone to this most suburban, safe experience. Maybe it wasn't even a piercing. Maybe it was a clip-on.

I got my coffee and decided to sit down inside to drink it. The sky was still dark and cloudy and could turn to rain again at any moment.

I watched with amusement as three girls, all about the age of 14 or 15 and traveling in a pack, came into the store. They were the new 14 or 15, not the 14 or 15 I grew up with, meaning they were the equivalent of 17 or 18 from the 1970s. Perfect, professionally-blonde and styled hair, emaciated bodies, and an apparent sharpness that came from knowing more about carnal desires than geopolitical conflict. If this sounds like a stereotype, I can't help it. These girls, and so many millions more just like them around the country, probably the world, are stereotypes. Their greatest goal is conformity, and their greatest fear is ostracization.

What the hell. If they'd taken one look at me, which they didn't, they would have quickly pigeonholed me, and they'd probably have been right. "Old guy, sitting alone, maybe a lech, but probably harmless. Hope I don't turn out like that."

The alpha wolf approached the counter first. Without acknowledging the "hello" or the smile of the woman behind the counter, Alpha started ordering.

"Triple tall non-fat latte, with one and a half Splendas," she said, staccato-like.

"Kendra!" squealed a trailing wolf. "Just get *half* a Splenda. You don't want to get fat or cancer or something."

Kendra the Alpha wolf reflexively clutched her concave belly. "Yeah," she said to the barista, "make it just one Splenda, not one and a half."

Ms. Eyebrow Piercing never smiled, except with her eyes. In a neutral tone of voice, she addressed Kendra.

"I could just open one packet of Splenda and sprinkle a few grains on your drink, if you'd prefer. That would be a 'triple tall non-fat latte with a Splenda sprinkle.'"

"Oh my God! You can do that?"

"Sure," Eyebrow said. Then she cut her eyes over to where I was sitting and offered a quick wink, and at that moment, I fell in love. I winked back, and I knew that Eyebrow and I were, even if only briefly, two connected human beings. The only thing that could spoil it is if we spoke to one another, so I finished my coffee and left, with a smile on my face.

The skies opened up again on my drive home, but when you're snug in a heated car, and streetlights and headlights are softly illuminating the late afternoon, a heavy rain is welcome. I didn't even worry about how flooded the golf course might become in the deluge because I knew I would have little, if any, chance to play before the election.

My car threw a spray of water as I turned onto my street, then into my driveway, and I was surprised to see Loren's car already there.

"Wow," I said, entering the kitchen where Loren was standing, going through the mail, "I didn't expect to see the woman of the house here quite yet."

Loren gave me a smile that was as warm and soft as the car ride I'd just taken. It may not be the most elegant image, but when she smiled like that, I thought of a crackling fire. Beautiful, but dangerously hot.

"And whom were you expecting?" Loren asked. She told me that a meeting at the store had finished early, and Ingrid had taken Elizabeth shoe shopping. Elizabeth had been asking for several days if she could have "just one pair of beautiful shoes." None of us knew what would fit that category, and why none of her present inventory made the grade, but Elizabeth promised Ingrid that she would know the right shoes when she saw them. It is a sign of having been married so many years, and of having an older sister, that I hadn't even questioned my daughter's reasoning.

So I'm proud to say that Loren and I were smart enough, and in love enough, to do what lovers should do when presented with the opportunity. The rain continued, now hitting the skylight in the hallway outside our bedroom, and for a few exquisite moments my bride and I were young again and alone in the world.

After, Loren asked me about my meeting with Hildy, and when I told her what happened, she smiled in a way that made me think she wanted to go another round. I was trying to determine what I had left in me (reminding myself that I was not, in fact, young again) when I realized I'd misinterpreted my wife's expression. This was a smile of loving approval, not encouragement, as such.

"I'm proud of you, Norman," Loren said, sounding formal in using my full name. "I'm not sure I would have done the same, but I figured you would. You should be proud of you, too."

It wasn't pride I felt, necessarily, but weariness.

"I guess so," was all I could muster in response, before dozing off.

CHAPTER TWENTY SIX

And finally it was Election Day.

About a week previously, I told Jeff that I declined to run around the county making last minute appearances in front of half a dozen Kiwanis or Lions who had already made up their minds on which straight ticket they would vote (usually Republican). It wasn't worth it, and I had difficulty appealing to such groups anyway.

"People always tell you to just be yourself, but they don't really mean that," is how I'd put it to Jeff on the phone.

"Well," Jeff had said, "that advice assumes that who you really are is likeable. In your case, you probably shouldn't be yourself. No offense."

"None taken. It's just that I get so tired of hearing people say, 'I support so-and-so because he seems like the kind of guy I'd like to have a beer with.' Fuck beer. How about voting for someone because they'll do the best job?"

"Yeah," Jeff said, "but the thing is, people don't understand the job, whether it's president or district judge. They won't take the time to learn the issues, so they try to trust their guts. It's a shortcut, and it could work okay except that the experts have figured out how to spin their candidates to make them seem more personally appealing, so it confuses the gut. I mean, come on, there are millions of Americans who think Reagan really did play football at Notre Dame with Rockne, when he wasn't sleeping with a chimp."

That made sense, but I protested to Jeff that I'd be a fun guy to have a beer with. Why couldn't strangers see that about me?

"Sorry, buddy," said Jeff. "You'd be a fun guy to have a good cabernet with, but I don't see you chugging down a Coors from the can."

"Jesus, is that's what's required?"

"See what I mean?" Jeff asked.

So I decided that there wasn't much I could do in the last week before the election to sway the results anyway, short of getting drunk at every redneck bar in Dallas County in seven days. And Jeff was right, I wouldn't fool anyone. Besides, it's not like Hildy was a laugh riot, either. Jeff did point out, pulling no punches, that a female candidate just needed to look like the kind of "good woman" who'd take a guy in with no questions asked after he'd gotten plastered and in a fistfight the night before.

Meanwhile, back at the courthouse, I was walking down a hallway in that last week before the big vote and saw Hildy emerging from Judge Curtis' office. They were both laughing about something, and Curtis had his bony Grim Reaper hand on Hildy's equally sharp shoulder, shellacked as it was in a carapace of navy blue coat. How cozy.

Hildy had the decency to look flustered when she saw me, but Curtis just grinned in his skull-enhanced way and nodded at me.

"Mr. Spiczek, how good to see you. We don't see you enough at the courthouse."

"Perhaps I'll be here more often in the near future," I said, nodding at Hildy as I passed.

Yes, I thought, I'll need to completely remodel Curtis' office. In fact, I'd switch courtrooms with someone if I could.

And his parking card for the judge's garage would need to be revoked immediately. Sometimes, if no one noticed or said anything, a retired judge would keep his parking privileges indefinitely and would continue to use the judges-only garage to come visit with his old friends. Curtis wouldn't so much have friends at the courthouse, but he might still like to haunt the place. He could do so from the public parking garage. These are the kinds of petty thoughts we all have (I think) and usually know enough to keep to ourselves.

Mostly, though, when I wasn't thinking directly of Hildy, I was ambivalent about the election. The newspaper ran a feature article on the Sunday before the Tuesday election saying that while Democrats had done well in the County in the previous election, polls were trending the Republicans' way this time. So I lowered my expectations, much the way I would do as a kid watching the Cowboys play. I told myself that if the players didn't actually trip on their shoelaces and break their legs as they ran onto the field, I should count that as a victory and expect no more. Then, any little success, or avoidance of failure, should be a pleasant surprise.

It didn't work out that way, though, not when I was a kid. Inevitably, I let myself get caught up in the game and lay my heart right out there on the rug in front of the console TV, exposing it to the puncture of televised cleats.

So in those few days of early November before the election, I simply went to my office and handled my cases like I always had. The only odd thing was when I had to get a hearing set in a case and would look at the calendar two months away. Would I still be practicing law then, I wondered? Should I keep reminding my clients that I may not be here for them if I won the election? I had told most of my clients that my withdrawal from their cases was possible but that they'd be in excellent hands with my associate if that happened. Some of the clients, I think, felt a vicarious little thrill that their lawyer might be a judge, but others just thought of the inconvenience to themselves, and I couldn't blame them. Switching lawyers in the middle of a case was more than just inconvenient, it could change the complexion of a case, and not always for the better.

When Jeff had convinced himself, by 10:00 a.m. on the morning of the election, that I truly would not attend the Democratic "get-out-the-vote" phone bank being run by Walter Stokely, he suggested we relax by playing golf. I went for that.

On the course an hour later, Jeff said, "You know, it'll really piss off Stokely and his minions that you aren't there today."

"How will you be able to tell?" I asked.

"I don't know," Jeff grunted as he hauled himself out of his cart and to the second tee box. "His glasses might steam up or something."

Jeff and I had both carded pars on the first hole, but I wasn't about to get my hopes up about this round. I've seen plenty of early success on a golf course turn to manure by the end of nine holes.

Exhibiting his usual disdain for gravity and physics, Jeff swung his club balletically (in the sense of a circus bear in a tutu) and pipelined a drive at least 250 yards down the heart of the fairway. As he posed in his follow through, Jeff glanced at the women's tees that sat at least 40 yards ahead of us.

"Jeez, the ladies sure have an advantage on this hole. Look where their damn tee box is."

Jeff lowered himself to the ground to pick up his tee, heaved himself back upright, and continued talking as I prepared to hit my own drive. I tried to concentrate on my setup and ignore him.

"You know," he said, still standing on the tee box about six feet behind me, "I don't know why all women aren't lesbians. I sure would be if I were a chick."

My jaw clenched, and I gripped the club tighter in my fingers. I went through my mental pre-swing checklist and swung the club.

Ah, yes, it was the glorious non-feeling of solid contact. My ball, like Jeff's, shot straight down the fairway, although not quite as far as his.

"Nice drive," Jeff said. He didn't speak again until we'd both approached our golf balls, a few feet apart, and I took a practice swing behind my ball.

"So what about you?" Jeff asked. "Wouldn't you want to be a dyke, too?" He asked this question like it was the most reasonable thing in the world to say.

I turned to look at him, my club in my hand.

"That's the stupidest damn question I've ever heard you ask, and that's saying a lot. Presumably, if you were a woman, chances are you'd like men, except there is some small chance you could be gay. Who the hell knows?"

I turned back to my ball and prepared to swing.

"So you'd do it with a *guy*?" Jeff seemed aghast.

I swung hard, too hard, and although I advanced the ball well, my shot was offline and the ball landed in a sand trap a good 20 feet in front of the green.

"Jesus," I barked at Jeff. "What is it with you?"

"Hey, look, I know you're tense about the election, man. I'm just trying to make conversation." Jeff shook his head at my outburst and dropped his second shot onto the front of the green.

And so it went, for 17 holes. I continued to play well, and Jeff continued what was mostly a monologue to distract me. In the course of three and a half hours, not only did he declare that he would be a lesbian if he were a woman, but he described also how he would dress as this hypothetical lesbian. He was okay with slacks, but he wouldn't be afraid to wear a dress. (I asked him how much he would weigh as a lesbian, and I received what I think was intended to be a hurt look).

No way would he get married, though, not even a civil union.

"What's the point of being gay if you have to get married like everyone else?" he asked.

And somehow, as we approached the 18th hole, Jeff and I were tied. I checked the sky for rain, then lightening, and even scanned for locusts and frogs. Nothing.

We both sailed drives down the right side of the fairway, and as we approached our shots into the green, Jeff finally acknowledged what was happening.

"I think you're gonna break through today, big guy," Jeff said to me. "This could be your day, at the polls and at the golf course. Hell, you've got me on the ropes."

"I know what you're doing," I replied. "You're trying to jinx me."

And when I landed my second shot on the green, about five feet from the hole, I turned to Jeff and said, "It won't work today."

True enough, it didn't work. Jeff put his second shot in a bunker and managed to finish with a bogie. I missed my putt, but still got a par. I had beaten Jeff by one stroke.

Jeff shook my hand on the 18th green.

"Congratulations, Mr. Spiczek. It wasn't me you beat, it was yourself. This game is always played against yourself."

The drive home didn't seem quite as traffic-clogged as it usually did, and I slid through the exit from LBJ to the Tollway without incident. Driving through there, though, did cause me to reflect on my decision, made a year ago, to run for judge. I'm not sure what my motivations were then, but I know they'd changed by now.

When I got home, Loren wasn't there yet. Elizabeth informed me that I was a "stinky daddy" and needed to take a shower, which I assured her I would do. Humilty is only a five-year-old away. Ingrid was planning to stay late with Elizabeth so that Loren and I could be at a Holiday Inn suite on one of our fair city's many freeways to host an election night party for a few of my bigger supporters and friends. I had intentionally kept it a small affair, thinking that, win or lose, I would probably not want to perform for a lot of strangers.

I emerged from a long, hot shower to see my beautiful wife zipping up her sexiest little black dress.

"Hey, are you ready?" Loren asked.

"Sure. What did you have I mind?"

"Ha. Come on, you don't want to be late for your own party. You know," Loren continued, "it was pretty exciting to vote for you this morning at the elementary school. I overheard a couple of women talking outside the school after I voted, and they were asking each other if they knew anything about any of the judicial candidates. So I walked right up to them and told them they should vote for my husband. One of them repeated your last name a couple of times to make sure she had it right, and I think both of them intended to vote for you."

"Well, that's sweet of you," I said. "I hope those are the two votes I need to put me over."

Loren turned to me and kissed me, careful not to get her dress wet because I hadn't dried off yet.

"You know what?" she asked. "I think you're going to win."

"You know what?" I responded. "I already have."

Made in the USA